THE SILENCE

THE SILENCE

A NOVEL

Karen Lee White

EXILE
editions

Publishers of Singular
Fiction, Poetry, Nonfiction, Translation, Drama and Graphic Books

Library and Archives Canada Cataloguing in Publication

White, Karen Lee, 1956-, author
The silence : a novel / Karen Lee White.

Accompanied by 1 CD-ROM of music attached to inside cover.
Issued in print and electronic formats.
ISBN 978-1-55096-794-4 (softcover).--ISBN 978-1-55096-795-1
(EPUB).--ISBN 978-1-55096-796-8 (Kindle).--ISBN 978-1-55096-797-5 (PDF).

I. Title.

PS8645.H5425S55 2018   C813'.6   C2018-905734-3
                                               C2018-905735-1

Text and music copyright © Karen Lee White, 2018
Book design by Michael Callaghan
Cover and CD artwork by Mark Preston
Typeset in Janson Text at Moons of Jupiter Studios

Published by Exile Editions Limited – www.ExileEditions.com
144483 Southgate Road 14 – GD, Holstein, Ontario, N0G 2A0
Printed and bound in Canada by Marquis
Second printing, 2019

We gratefully acknowledge the Canada Council for the Arts,
the Government of Canada, the Ontario Arts Council,
and the Ontario Media Development Corporation
for their support toward our publishing activities.

Canadian sales representation:
The Canadian Manda Group, 664 Annette Street,
Toronto ON M6S 2C8 www.mandagroup.com 416 516 0911

North American and international distribution, and U.S. sales:
Independent Publishers Group, 814 North Franklin Street,
Chicago IL 60610 www.ipgbook.com toll free: 1 800 888 4741

When I am silent, I have thunder hidden inside.
—RUMI

I yearn for silence as some might hunger after wine; ache for a lover's touch. An early explorer, I happened one August upon my first silence in the far North. Stepping onto the gravel of the Alaska Highway in sun-burned air one early morning in a wild place, in the dry. A strange still-ness not heard before, a ceaseless buzzing, humming. Willing myself to hear the deep quiet, the nothingness, I could not. The first perfect hush I did hear seduced my being. It was disquieting, holy.

In time I learned to surrender without fear. Allow quiet to seep, seek into my deep. To be perfectly still within silence, embrace it, cherish it.

I seek silence, discover it rarely, and always unforeseen. It is almost extinct.

It lives between a raven's calls that echo through cedar-fragrant rain forest. By a still lake on Kwakwaka'wakw lands – Before, then After – the logging trucks growl and mutter by. In the smothering of a Coastal fog. In the middle of the night, between dog barks. Silence lives in the between. This is where the Old Ones speak, and I can hear. In the silence. In the space between.

MOON OF THE WITCH

Someone talkin' in my head quiet with a kick like rhyme
And I know it's you
And feeling half-crazy I smile in the dark
Can't deny you got me good 'cause I know it's true
Chorus:
And it's not really fair, no it's not really fair, oh it's hardly fair
You're not really there...

Chapter One

In a way, dead Indians are just like live ones. They have senses of humour, they like to tease. Even get a person in hot water. They steal my stuff. Like yesterday. I was late, searching for my phone. It vanished from where I knew I'd just left it. I made a frantic search of the house. In case I was mistaken, which I knew damned well I wasn't. Nothing. Then, there it was in the same spot, in plain sight, placed exactly as I thought I had left it. They always do that, it's like their punchline. Be so frustrating. They ask for things like tea with sugar, and weird food – Kentucky Fried Chicken, Pepsi and jelly beans.

I'm Leah.

I grew up thinking I was poor white trash. When I was fifteen, I cornered my father who confessed that we were Indian, like it was a crime. So, if I was a poor Indian, at least that was a reason for being poor.

I went to Whitehorse at nineteen and hooked up with "Haywire." My first boyfriend. He was one of the first real Indians I'd ever met. You know, the ones that always knew they were Indians. That didn't know hiding it or being ashamed were options. I sure let Dad know. And, he wasn't happy. Bonus Bingo!

Haywire's mother, Doris, was the only person that called him "Arthur." All the Charlies in the family lived at Little Annie Lake. It's a ways out of Whitehorse, off the highway.

The first winter, Haywire and I stayed out in the bush to trap. I started having visits from the dead folks.

Don't be impressed that I trapped. The only thing we got all winter was a squirrel's foot. The squirrel left his foot behind. Chewed off his own foot to get away. Either that or the rest of him was eaten by a coyote. That's what Uncle Angus said. I feel awful about it to this day. Uncle Angus taught us to trap. He said it wasn't our fault we didn't get anything because that winter was one big Chinook and the animals didn't need our trap bait.

We got no fur, but I learned a lot – to listen the instant I heard an unexpected gunshot off in the distance, for a "doof" at the end to know a bullet had hit an animal. And I could tell how many guns were going off. Like people, each gun has its own voice. I discovered the "Indian phone." It's when you put out that you want to see someone, and not long later they show up. And if you ask if they "got your Indian phone call," they always say "Yes."

Bush people are good at that.

When you show up they already have tea made and fresh bannock ready.

They say, "Oh, so that was *you* that was coming." You can't surprise them; they just know someone is going to show up.

Gramma Maisey used to motion to the stove and say "Tea deh" in her Tagish accent as sweet as her tea. When I first showed up at Little Annie, Haywire and I had gone to visit one or two of the Charlies at their houses for tea. I'm so light-skinned they thought I was white. *"Bring that Kutchen over so we can check her out,"* his aunties told him. He would grin. I guess he thought my long black hair would be a giveaway to who I really am. What I didn't know then was that he'd never brought a girl home. So, it was a big deal.

Haywire's Mom didn't seem to like me. It wasn't anything personal. No woman was good enough for her boy.

She did save my life once, though.

The first dead guys who came in a dream were Haywire's two uncles. They were kind enough to introduce themselves, but I knew their names already. Alfred and Arthur Charlie. Almost every day Haywire said how much he missed them. We hung around and had tea. Just like the live relatives I had met one by one in the cabins that snugged up to Little Annie Lake.

Those uncles asked all kinds of questions about my family. About where I came from, how I grew up. I was confused. I'd always thought spirits knew everything already.

℘

ME AND NO ONE IN THE RAIN

I remember laughing, I remember talking
I remember running, slowing then and walking
Neon lights floating on puddle water
Shushing of the cars, the buzzing of the wires
Painted lady waiting on the corner
Shooting sentimental glances my way
I'm all alone but it really doesn't matter
I could swear it doesn't matter
Me and no one in the rain
Me and no one in the rain

℘

Looking far past her reflection in the plane window, she recalled how Haywire looked back then and smiled. He had kept his hair short; his hands seemed separate from him. He was always tidying the front of his hair, using his fingers as a comb – that lock forever dropping into his face, the softer black of half-breed hair. He was neither dark-skinned nor light. Indians knew he was Native, but white people couldn't tell until he opened his mouth. The Tagish accent, the dropping of letters at the end of words, was a dead giveaway. It was one of the many things that she had fallen in love with.

A bush Indian who knew everything about that land. With a gentle, slow, sweet smile that lit up those dark eyes. But, as the Tagish would say, he could really "hold a mean." His temper was something else. Leah wondered how he looked now that he was older. If that fire between them would still smoulder? That kind of passion between two people was a once in a lifetime gift. She grinned about them making love in the bush when they were supposed to be hunting. After, he would say how dangerous that was in bear country, that bears were attracted by the smell of love-making. Neither had cared. What would he be like now, and what would the North be like to her after all these years? She had met him at nineteen. The blush of youth was gone after two decades.

That winter they had trapped was hard, but how she had loved it! The first and only time she had felt alive. Not like now. These days she existed. Her thoughts turned to Phillip. She loved him but knew without having to be told that it was over. They just hadn't said the words. Something had prevented her from marrying him, but she had committed herself for five gruelling years. It was exhausting. The condo with white-on-white everything down to the couch. His inability to relax around her Indigenous friends, family. It was worse that she had to be a civil servant and a professional Indian offering counsel on everything that others should learn themselves. What kind of gift was it appropriate to give to a Nation? How should they acknowledge traditional territory in meetings? What was a good frybread recipe? Could they go to a powwow? Could they attend a big house ceremony? She longed for the music she had long left behind. But Phillip was kind, treated her respectfully. It was clear he would never grasp the culture, but she felt cared for. He wasn't affectionate but was a great lover in that he tried. He was white and uptight, after all. She grinned at herself in the window, took a sip and allowed the cool water to trickle slowly down her throat.

Ah, being held by Native men. Man, when they held you it was as if their heart and soul were in their arms, hands, and bodies. With a touch they could melt your defences like cold butter on hot bannock. Haywire was the best lover she'd ever had. He had stroked her all over her body each time, as if he were a musician playing a beautiful instrument. She had never tired of the music his hands spoke to her skin, eloquent erotic poetry beyond words. She had thought of his touch a thousand times since. How he had somehow known what her skin longed for. That yearning never left her. A deeper sensual heat arose at the thought of his hands wandering the open terrain of her body.

Damn, she thought, *that's just wrong that he was the first. Why couldn't my last lover be the most intimate?*

ॐ

DANCE AWAY

Longing has new meaning, yearning has new meaning
I long and I yearn and yet as you asked
as I promised I have kept you with me
while you dance away
I swear to you I saw us take a tear from each other's eyes
and put it in our mouths

and the tears became diamonds
and then many diamonds that fell from our mouths
and you danced away

I see you and you see me
I hear you and you hear me
You know me and you cause me
to be a witness to my beauty
without fear and without shame
And I hold this all within me,
tenderly knowing
that you will dance away

CHAPTER TWO

"Haywire!" she yelled, dropping her carry-on bags, running out of the heat into icy air. She was full of the heady excitement of a longed-for reunion. She almost knocked him off his feet, embracing and kissing him on a cold cheek.

"Holeeee, woman, you tryin' out for the B.C. Lions?" She heard the laughter fill his voice. "Easy, easy."

"Oh, my God, Haywire – look at you – you're a sexy old man," she laughed, punching him on the arm. "Why is it?"

"Why is what?"

"That men with grey hair look so damned sexy – women just look…old."

Haywire grinned. She was almost the old Leah. Almost. More beautiful than ever. But there was that lost look deep in her eyes. He busied himself with her luggage.

"Come on, Chaos. Uncle won't wait forever."

She laughed at her forgotten nickname from the days of Haywire and Chaos. It was a slow sweet embrace. She flushed despite the frigid air. He led her to a light blue and white '56 Chevy truck.

"Hooooooleh! Still have this ole wreck? Ever fix the bullet holes?"

"Nope, kept 'em for souvenirs."

"Some souvenirs. The RCMP trying to kill you?"

"Somethin' to tell the grandkids." He glanced at her as he hefted her suitcase.

"Lord Geezus, woman, you got rocks in this case?"

The truck had that old-vehicle smell she loved. Old leather. And the faint smell of oil.

"Gonna stop for smokes before we go to the hospital." He fired up the engine. Leah smiled enjoying the familiar deep-throated growl. The tires squeaked as they moved through the snow.

"You're still sucking on those coffin nails?"

"No," he said "the smokes'd be for you. You're kinda tense." She gave him another gentle slap, knowing he was teasing her. "How long has Uncle been sick?"

"Dunno, never said nothing. I had the dream four months back."

She waited for him to explain. He didn't need to. He stopped and said, "I'll be back."

"Consider me placated," she replied.

"What lingo is that? He looked annoyed as he slammed the door. She knew it was a dig about using "city words." With a grade seven mission school education, he thought she was flaunting.

They crossed the bridge spanning the Yukon River. Their ability to hold a comfortable silence made it seem as though no time had passed at all. Under streetlights the snow was tinged a pathetic pink-yellow. Leah recognized the parking lot, the low building. Nothing had changed in twenty-five years.

"Truck, truck, car, truck, truck, truck," she said, trying to be light.

"What?"

"Obviously the North – all the trucks."

He gave her a quick glance but didn't respond. He was gathering himself. She remembered this about him, how at home he was in the bush, awkward in town. He slammed the door. Squared up. Lit a smoke. Took a few hard drags, threw it down. Stepped on it hard.

"Let's make tracks," he said.

Sliding doors, the warm blast of hospital air. That odour she could not bear. Infirm humans and disinfectant. She trembled. Emotions swam like circling sharks. What was wrong with her? It wasn't about Uncle Angus, it was that hospital stink. Haywire stopped short at Uncle's door.

"He's gone," was all he said.

"He's sleeping," not believing her own words.

"Yes, he is, but he isn't ever going to wake up."

Haywire stood motionless looking down. The brown face, lined, the colour of smoked moose hide, hair all shades of grey. The lean body looked tiny. The spirit gone from the shell left behind in the bed. Haywire felt his presence and knew that he had not gone yet. His chest painfully tight, he could barely breathe. Unshed tears locked behind his eyes.

Leah wailed as Haywire stood silent. She had no sense of how long they stayed, but Leah knew she was crying Haywire's tears.

❧

Angus Charlie is walking soundlessly though the meadows on moccasin-covered feet. He has just turned ten years old, is finally allowed to hunt alone. Happy to be out on this shimmering fall day, raven wings *whoh*, *whoh*, and *whoh* just above his head. Smiling at the wing beats, he imitates them perfectly. The golden light and long shadows of late afternoon. The brilliant blue of the sky intensified by white clouds, slowly travelling to the south on a steady breeze.

All signs point to the moose having come down from the hills for the rut. He has seen the branches where they have scraped velvet from antlers. The larger game will be moving this time of day. This is his first hunt alone and everything is alive to him. His hearing is sharp, his eyes picking up all colours, shape, movement. He will intuit energy before seeing or hearing animals. He carefully carries his father's .22 in his hand, the .30-30 over his left shoulder.

The path he follows is an old one his family has always walked, to the meadows. The huge flat in this valley has been part of the family trapline for generations. A squirrel whirrs alarm at his approach. He stands still until silence falls once more. Until there is only the *sshhhh* of drying leaves rising with the breeze, all the gold leaves in that great meadow speaking to one another, the grass answering. The sound rises and falls, rises and falls in slow waves, north to south.

Angus stands straight like any of the trees. He has no fear, this is his home. He knows where the bears will be, the wolverines. How to respectfully address them if they cross paths. Passing a grove of pine his eyes go to the tree where his sister birthed her first child. The trees share one root among them, like a family. His family. He looks to the place where he will set rabbit snares with Father when the snow comes. He sniffs the air. He smells the sun-bleached grass, the alders, the tang of spruce pitch.

He senses the moose and searches for it now, amongst the next group of trees. For the tell-tale rust between the glowing silver-white trunks. He arcs around to a clearing on the other side. Behind a tree he waits. He barely catches the muted sound of distant voices on the breeze. Haywire? Leah? But they have not been born yet! Momentarily distracted, his single focus is on the animal. This is the most magnificent cow moose he has ever laid eyes on. He admires her raw, wild beauty. Flawless, except for an old wound on her left back flank where the hair does not grow. He and the animal breathe the same autumn-scented air the trees have exhaled. Closing his eyes, he feels his heart beating, slow, steady, senses her heartbeat. Feels her life force enter him.

Leah somewhere now, sobbing as if her heart is broken. He wills his focus back to the creature. Opens his eyes, swings the .30-30 to line up the open sight. He knows it's bent. It must be a perfect shot. He has one bullet. The animal must not suffer or run. Angus senses Haywire, as surely as if he is standing there at his side. He hears the wailing, wants to comfort Leah. Instead, he takes a breath, holds it, fires. Thunder, thud, crashing of brush. The moose does not attempt to rise, he sees her flank rise and fall with quick breaths. He will let her be for a time. Allow her to die alone, in peace. He allows the oneness with all that is to fill him, as he has been taught. He thanks the animal for giving her life to feed his family and allows gratitude to fill him. Feels her heart slowing, begins to mentally prepare for skinning and butchering.

Someone. A flash of movement beyond his vision. Father, grandfather, coming across to him, their long shadows moving just ahead of them, the shadows of great birds. He sees their smiles of pride, his father waves. They are close now, and he knows it is time, does not hesitate to go to meet them. Together they will fly home.

୧୨

SOMEONE ELSE IS DRIVING

When someone else is driving you can close your eyes
If the sun is shining, you can see your own designs

Pinwheel warriors in a fire-orange sky
When someone else is driving and you close your eyes
When someone else is driving and you close your eyes

When I close my eyes, I can see what I want
Don't ask for nothing you won't get what you want
Only what comes to you and only what's there
Fall into the mystic if you dare

CHAPTER THREE

Leah woke alone at dawn in erotic damp, her body on fire with want for Haywire. Shoulders bare, she shivered in the chilly air. They had shared a room at the Old North Hotel. At ease with each other, it had seemed strange to sleep in separate beds. She knew he had remembered the intimate nights they had spent here. She felt no guilt about her attraction, but it had surprised her with its intensity. After all this time.

He was sitting at the small burn-scarred Formica table, waiting for her. In fact, he had been sleepless the entire night, wanting her, fighting his need to join her. To stroke her skin until she begged for him as she always had.

"Come on, Chaos, we have a ways to go."

"Get me coffee if you want me to go anywhere."

She watched him walk out the door, how he filled out his jeans and jean jacket. His long strides in those cowboy boots. *Damn*, she thought, *there's something hot about an Indian man in cowboy boots*. She lay in bed, trying to cool her thoughts about him. After some time, she forced herself to get up and into the shower. *Crap!* She'd forgotten her shampoo. Leaving the shower running, she stepped naked on wet feet into the room.

"That my reward for the coffee?" She heard Haywire's drawl, saw him caressing her body with his eyes, toes to head. Outside air hit her and her nipples hardened.

"Shut up and give it to me."

"I'm married," he laughed in his quiet way, shaking his head. She felt the heat again, knew the lust in her voice betrayed her and flushed. Acting as cool as she could, she sighed and boldly crossed to him, and took the coffee from his outstretched hand.

"Rrrrrrr," she growled; "I'm talking about the coffee!"

"Cream, no sugar," he said, sweet smile, head down. She was not fooled. "You remembered?"

"Couldn't forget that body."

That made her want to walk to him, put her arms around his neck and kiss him hot. Instead, she took a sip and spat it back in the Styrofoam cup.

"What's the matter?"

"It's not Starbucks, that's what's wrong with it." He shook his head. Smiled that little boy smile.

"You're welcome. Best I could do. Free from the lobby."

"Crap coffee." She tried to slam the bathroom door behind her to make a point, but infuriatingly, it was one of those light-weight pressurized doors you couldn't get a decent slam out of. Not a drum. Not by a long shot.

Once outside in the slick parking lot, Leah gripped Haywire's arm. The truck was ice-cold. Haywire adjusted the choke. The engine caught. Haywire let it warm up. He motioned to a small box between them.

"Uncle said to give that to you." She looked at Haywire without speaking. Opening it, she sucked her breath in.

"No way," she laughed. "I'd forgotten all about these things!" She picked up a Super 8 reel.

"Oh yeah, your movie."

"Documentary," she corrected, missing his dancing eyes. "I'll have to watch these again, see what's on them."

"Everybody in the Charlie family you pestered with questions like some cheechako." Haywire was grinning. She felt a little defensive.

"Your family didn't mind."

"Nobody could say no to you, that's all to it."

She read out the labels on the films, one by one. *All to it.* She had always corrected him with "all there *is* to it." He was doing it on purpose. Playing up the bush-Indian speak. She ignored him this time.

"Gramma, Uncle Angus, Auntie Laylie..." Her eyes ached from tears that would not fall. A small, fat, hide-covered book.

"What's this?" she asked, more to herself. It was covered with thick brain-tanned moose hide. Embellished with Northern-style beadwork.

"That diary I was so jealous of."

"I don't remember this, this isn't mine." Something. Not right. Something.

"You drove me nuts writing in that thing. You don't remember us fighting over it?"

"I *don't*," she was hot with annoyance. Now she felt numb, her ears ringing. She turned it over to look at the plain back.

"I don't remember this at all." Foreboding. Creeping up from her icy feet. "Haywire, this isn't funny. Why would you say this's mine?" She heard the distress in her own voice. The roar to rumble as the truck passed from asphalt and hit chip seal.

He did not speak as they drove out to Little Annie. She sensed what she had almost forgotten. The rhythms of this ancient scape. A land unspoiled, breath-taking. Spruce trees, tall and narrow from base to tip. Standing in a carpet of snow like tall graceful Tlingit ladies with long skirts.

A gravel road ahead, mountains rising out of the foothills on either side. She knew them well. Calm settled in her belly like a resting cat.

The sky a brilliant blue, dusty clouds unmoving. With deep cold, it was always dead still. High up, the trees were navy blue. An indication of how cold it was up high. Haywire had taught her to see those things.

Peaks stretching, reaching their slate-grey heads out of quilts of snow. The sun touching peaks, shadows that clung to the sides like shy children.

Leah tasted the exhaled breath of the mountains. Stone voices whispered to her blood. Blood to stone, stone to skin, bone to stone.

"No wonder I wrote so many songs here – the raw beauty, to feel a small part of creation."

"Yeah, Chaos, you wrote some good ones."

The engine stopped, and they rolled slowly to a stop. She had forgotten that air-cooled engines could freeze without warning.

The first time it had happened, years ago, she had panicked. She had not been dressed warmly. Haywire and his cousin had just stared at her when she had asked what the hell they were going to do. Not understanding, they had sat quietly for long minutes as the cold stole in and her anxiety had mounted. Then, Haywire had started the truck, and they had carried on.

Now, she waited for Haywire to start up the engine. Instead, he jumped out. The clang of the door in the deep silence startled her. She caught the whiff of cigarette smoke. The engine fired on the first turn of the key. They drove in silence. This was the way of Northern people, not needing words, voices, to communicate. Their silence spoke for them. City people, she knew, would be unnerved by this. She slipped into it, relaxed.

Peaceful with Haywire, it seemed as though nothing had ever gone wrong between them. He intuited her thoughts. He glanced at a photograph on the dashboard, then at her. His family. His way of telling her that things had changed, he was married. Had kids, a life. Her throat tightened. He reached out, gently took her hand, saying what he would never say with words. Then, he did speak.

"There hasn't been a day since I met you that I have not said your name."

"I love you too, Haywire, always did. I will always remember that." Their words hung, fired heat in the frosty air of the truck all the way to Little Annie.

CHAPTER FOUR

Instinct willed the cow moose to lie very still in the pasture despite the pain that tore through her body. Emitting low rumbles in her throat, imperceptible except to the ravens watching from the tree above, her swollen belly heaved with yet another involuntary contraction. Her body powerfully tensed. Coursing muscles working to expel the life within her. The enormous pressure was not released by the waves of blindingly unbearable throbbing. Between she would sniff, to catch the scent of any enemies that might find her easy prey; although she would not be able to flee. She had chosen a spot long before this began, where she could see in all directions.

The light of midday stretched into the long light and shadow of late day. It was time. With difficulty she struggled to her feet, squatting at the back legs. The final purge, her entire body with nothing to do but expel a life from within to without. The pressure, the spasmodic agony as it moved lower, lower still. Through her torment, she heard the baby land behind her back legs. Tremoring from the exertion of hours, she turned to see the tiny being behind her, still encased in a milky white sac. Bending on tired legs, she began to lick and nose the caul to free the calf. Too weak to stand, it feebly mewled as it caught the scent of her teats. She lapped its tiny body from head to tail to stimulate circulation before allowing it to eat. Energy from the nutrients in the liquid surged through her body, driving the weakness from her.

Yet too weak to stand, the calf pointed with its damp head toward the smell of her teats. The cow felt her milk flow down to engorge her udders. Still, the tiny one did not stand and nurse. By now it should have sucked its fill, falling a few times on new legs. She nuzzled her encouragement; pushed with her nose. There was terrible danger: predators would be hunting in the long shadows of late day. The calf was listless, barely moved. It let out a weak sound as she sniffed it twice, nudged it three times.

There was no use to wait. She moved away to a safer place to bed for the night. The little one should have been trotting behind, now on sure legs. Instead, it lay abandoned, quivering in the cold, growing chilled. It would not survive predators. The cow reached a dense thicket. She was hungry, having fasted during the long hours of the birth. She found willows to satiate her hunger. A half-hour away, where low golden light now weakly touched the tops of trees, the calf tremored one last time, stilled.

Coyote caught the scent. Trotting, tail up, he made ready to scavenge an easy prey.

CHAPTER FIVE

In the cool, stark light and shadow of afternoon a coyote gives birth. The last kit does not come easily. When it is finally born, the mother licks him as the other six feed. He breathes weakly, and she nudges his chest with her head. With a weak leg, this one will not stand. After their first feeding, it's time to move the whelps deeper into the warmth of the den. She nudges all but the lame one as they lurch to their feet. She moves them, one by one, patiently. The lame pup tries to follow his family, repeatedly falling. His mother does not wait.

He flounders up, falls again. He stands and trips. His lame leg is slower than his other three. Struggling again and again, his mother and the others disappear one by one. Whining and whimpering, his breath hangs in the glacial air. At last he succeeds. Exhausted, following the scent of his mother's milk, he falls several times, and fights back up. Stiff with cold when he catches up, he is shivering. The others are feeding again. He moves to latch on to a nipple. The mother pushes him away. Obsessed by the pain of hunger, he perseveres until he is no longer shoved off. Not much milk left by that time, he is left wanting, a burning ache in his belly.

By late spring, the kits are lively and growing. The lame one is smaller, due to scant milk but his leg is stronger. Ignored by his mother, he must come in and feed at the end each time. He slowly grows a little. He runs awkwardly behind the others. He's not welcomed to their rolling, nipping play or in the chasing of mice. He does this alone, off from the family.

As hunger constantly nags, he begins to hunt tiny prey. The kits feed at night and fall asleep together in a warm heap. He's stopped feeding from his mother, sleeps alone. He is safer in the den with the others; so he stays. Not bonded with the other kits, nor his mother, who nips him often to show he is not wanted. His cunning grows earlier, and he begins to live on rabbits. He is small but lean and strong from his good hunting. While the others still play he has learned to survive alone.

After the first dusting of snow, he is attacked by his brother kit as he enters the den. He fights with ferocity, sinks his fangs deep into the neck. Thick, dark-red blood pools on red-blond fur, drips, then streams to the earth. The pup seizures without sound. A triumphant runt feeds on his still warm brother. This is the night he leaves and does not return.

This is a wandering coyote who's much smaller than he should be. This is a coyote who is keen in sense and can live and fight on his own. This is a coyote who never will hunt in a pack. This is a coyote who will yip and cry to the moon alone. This is a coyote that has no home.

❧

Leah woke in the frigid dark. Confused, she checked her cell phone. 9:30 a.m. Saw only the sign of dawn through the window. It was weird, being in the dark so late in the morning. Throwing heavy covers off, squinting in the half-light, she made her way to the wood box she had helped Haywire to fill. He had insisted on cutting kindling, teasing her about being a city girl, not being able to make fire to save her life.

She felt a little nervous, knowing that her life now depended on fire. Grasping a sharp knife, as Uncle Angus had always done, she whittled a number of pieces of kindling so the curls, still attached, would catch easily. She placed them in the wood stove, leaving spaces for air, and lit a match, moved the sticks with the poker as they caught, to ensure the fire would take hold. She sighed with relief when the flames shone light into the dark of the cabin. She placed two larger blocks of wood on top, waiting for them to light before clanging the door closed.

From the road, Haywire saw the first tendrils of smoke in the still air crawl slowly out of the stovepipe. He said quietly to himself, "So the greenhorn still knows how to make fire." He had been about to sneak in and light it for her. He walked up the trail to his truck, smiling as he drove away.

Leah's ears caught the sound of the familiar engine fading in the distance. She smiled, knowing Haywire had been watching over her.

The fire was snapping, crackling and roaring, and she could take it no longer; she desperately needed to pee. Damned if she was going to use the slop bucket. She pulled on her jacket and Doris's old boots.

"Here goes," she said to herself and stepped outside, pulling the wood plank door closed until the latch caught. Forgetting cold, she was captured. Everything was white except the black of the trees. Crystal snow on twigs like iced fingers. Leah stood for a moment, turned left to the lake blanketed with thick snow. A restful sight for city-tired eyes. The sky above her lighting to a deep azure, as it can in the high North. Clouds still. So slow, she had to hold her eyes on one spot to see that they were actually moving. A million shades of grey. The mountains in the distance, pristine through clear air. Cloud hanging like smoke across their tops. They seemed to sit, looking at her, waiting with infinite patience. What were they waiting for? Peaks dusted with snow, veiled by cloud. Tree-covered sides sun-touched. The largest a grand old lady of all with a cloud veil, a shawl.

The breath was freezing in her nose. Throat dried, lungs rebelling against the dry cold, she coughed. She turned to look back at the cabin.

Yesterday, she and Haywire had walked out to the ice on the creek to chop a hole with an axe. He had pulled a bucket for her which now stood beside the stove. Leah looked around this place she had thought of so often during the years. She swore she heard Angus's voice:

"You gonna freeze?" She didn't bother to close the outhouse door. It didn't look as though it would. She sat, shivering, grateful for the Styrofoam seat, looking to where the creek met the lake remembering the sheltered spot where the little boat once sat, tied up to a tree, moving in the eddy when the weather was warm. Now, the old thing was up against the cabin on the lakeside. Only patches of aluminium showed through thick snow. Her eyes followed old animal tracks and she smiled at the flash of a magpie in a nearby tree. Her toes were cold pinched, and she walked faster as she approached the cabin. She kicked her boots against the door frame, knocking off snow.

The fragrance of smoke reminded her to check the fire. She added a larger piece of wood, enjoying the heat radiating from the ornate old stove. Long after Gramma and Uncle had moved to a new house a mile up the road, she remembered coming down with Haywire and finding Uncle here. They would knock and enter, find him content, solitary, forming fur stretchers with a knife, or cleaning traps.

There would be coffee and a cast-iron frying pan full of fragrant, freshly cooked fish. He had always said, "Made too much, help yourselves." She knew he did this on purpose. That whitefish was the most delicious fish she had ever eaten. It was because it was fresh caught. She tried always to cook it like Uncle, rolling it in flour, with only a little salt, frying it slowly in lard. It was never as delicious and crisp as his.

WAITING FOR THE GRACE TO FALL

You say I'm wise, can help you through
I've survived, yes that's true
But I can't speak
I have no words for you
I'm waiting without waiting
Like the Old Ones do
Waiting for the grace to fall…
You say I have no fear, that's not quite true
I just don't have the same fear as you
You cannot know, and I cannot get through
I'm listening without listening, afraid I may not hear
Listening for the grace to fall
Listening for the grace to fall

CHAPTER SIX

"Oh, my God, the meadows!" Leah grabbed Haywire's arm as they followed another familiar road.

"Easy, you want to dig us out of the ditch? Remember how we got to the trapline from this side?" Haywire was silent for a bit. He said softly, "After you left, I couldn't go there for two whole years."

Leah looked sideways at him. There was a lump in her throat. That was happening a whole lot here.

"That must have been hard. You loved that place, your guaranteed grouse hunting ground."

"Yep, Mom sure missed grouse. Hardly got them after that. She had to get used to rabbits." They both laughed, remembering Doris sighing, "Ah, this greazy old thing," her hints as hard as a whetstone; "Sure be nice to cook a nice fat grouse, but no, just this old rabbit...Ach." She always said that when they came in from the trapline with rabbits.

She'd fried the "greazy" rabbit in her treasured cast-iron pan like fried chicken and they had always enjoyed it noisily. Doris had loved it too but had to make her point. They had laughed about that in private. Sometimes, when Haywire came home with grouse in his pack, saying "Here, Mom, more rabbits," she would groan and roll her eyes. When he pulled out the birds, already plucked, her eyes would widen, her cheekbones would rise into her gap-toothed smile of pure delight.

"Sonny!" She would praise, in a soft voice, "you plucked it."

And each time he would reply, "Well, it's either I do it when it's still warm, or hear you moan how hard it is to pluck cold."

Leah had loved watching Doris pinch the feathers off birds. Her fingers like chubby tweezers, with a quick short motion that made a ripping sound when the feathers came out. She could pluck even a large bird clean in a few minutes flat. If the bird was legal, the feathers went into the dump behind the house. If not, they were buried off in the bush. Because, as she would say, "You never know when that Game Warder might come sniffin' around here." The Game Warder never showed in all three years Leah was around. Back then, land claims had yet to be settled. Bush Indians lived in fear of being fined for eating traditional foods, the ones on the "protected" list. The Charlies made up other names to call protected species, as if the Game Warder could hear Doris from miles out in the bush, talking about us going for "singers" (swans).

"Oh, my God, Haywire!" Leah's eyes were wide. That was the look he lived for. The tough city exterior was gone and uncertainty showed a little girl who really did need an old bush Indian.

"This village hasn't changed at *all!*"

He smiled.

"Are you sure those Wolf ladies are okay with me helping out with the cooking?" Haywire glanced at her: "Like I said the other three times, and now for all time – yes." Leah ignored the "all time."

"Those ladies are all yacking like magpies that you're coming to help them cook for Uncle's party."

Party meant potlatch. Angus was from the Ganaxteidi Crow Clan. Preparation for his last gathering was the Wolf Clan's cultural obligation. Sacred duty. Right up to the end of the funeral, they would be busy. Arranging and covering tables, setting up chairs in the school gym. The wild-food feast would be ready.

❧

The Clan leader began to call out in the language, commanding everyone's attention.

Haywire's elder cousin, Lorna, leaned to Leah and whispered in her ear. "He is calling on the Ganaxteidi ancestors, so they know Uncle Angus is coming." Leah knew, but nodded. The calling went on, and the crowd of close to one hundred stood very still, silent, watching, listening. Sun sparkled on snow.

Leah looked to the long-ago fences. Still standing, paint fading, some greyed to bare wood. There were many newer graves, with plastic flowers, strange against the snow. She imagined those flowers in the heat of summer, in rain, fall frost, the deep cold of winter, spring thaw.

The Chinook today felt warm on Leah's skin. It was good to have wakened in the cabin this morning without the frigid cold.

Leah focused on the words rolling off the tongue of the Speaker. She recognized the words, *"Gunałchish, Gunałchish, Gunałchish!"* People huddled closer to the grave as the coffin was unloaded with care from the back of Haywire's truck. The pallbearers stood, respectful.

Lorna whispered, "Walk with the family." Haywire's sister, Danielle, hugged her hard and kept her arm around her as they walked through the gate following the casket. The Charlies circled the gaping grave. Leah wondered how the gravediggers had burrowed through the permafrost.

As the Clan leader spoke in English of Angus's life, Leah wept soundlessly beside the wailing Charlie women. Haywire's face was down, but he did not cry. He glanced at Leah, then down to the coffin beside the grave. Leah looked at the simple pine box. She knew Haywire had made it with loving hands. There was a design on the top, carved in. She knew it: the view from the old cabin. A wail escaped, unheeded, and she heard it, and then recognized her own voice. Haywire looked at her hard, but she could not stop. All the Charlie women keened and cried, and Leah knew this was the way of it. The women cried for all the men who stood silent. Lorna began to sob as if she were singing, in long wails, up, then down. Leah thought of wolves that had keened the night before, miles off across the lake, in the dark. She had opened the door and walked out to listen. Lorna sounded like those wolves crying up, down, and up slow, and down slow. On and on she sang. When it was over Lorna touched Leah's arm.

"Come on, Leah. Let's go change before we head over to the Hall."

"How could you have known how much being with the family would mean to me?" Leah's voice trembled. Lorna smiled her gentle smile.

"You are one of us, now. You'll always be part of the Charlie family." Leah's heart kindled with both love and bittersweet memories.

☙

Lorna whistled when she saw Leah in black suede pants, black suede boots, and a flowing blouse of deep emerald green.

"Well, that oughta get Haywire's attention!"

At the Hall, a couple of women stood at a welcome table with different-coloured ribbons on tiny pins.

"Crow or Wolf?"

"Both Wolf," said Lorna, before Leah could answer. They were given pins with blue ribbons to put on. This was new to Leah, but it seemed practical. Not everyone had identifying clan vests or other regalia.

There was laughing, and joshing, tears for the departed loved one were left behind. This was the time to celebrate Uncle Angus's life. Leah had always treasured this tradition. The whole community sharing the burden of grief and then shifting the family to the joy of remembrance. Lorna led Leah to the Charlie family head table at the front. They passed through a sea of wide smiles, laughter, the shaking of hands, hugs, children chasing one another, the cooing of babies.

On her way back to the head table, Leah looked out at her adopted clan, the Wolf people. My, but they were beautiful, tall, proud, fierce. She recognized and stopped to shake hands with "The Singing Cowboy," Jim Tom, still tall and handsome. Unchanged after all these years. She saw many young faces she did not know but who seemed familiar. Older men still in their long-brimmed ball caps with company labels, wool plaid shirts with jeans or the dark green bush-style pants.

One by one, young people embraced Leah and said their names. It was as if Leah was collecting a basket of gifts from the other side. So many of their parents were gone now. Leah was moved to see children grown up, to know that their late parents still lived through them. To be greeted by them in such a happy and loving way was bittersweet, yet spirit-filling. She had the sweet feeling of belonging. How she had missed this!

The delicious aroma of wild food, plates of bumguts, a treasured delicacy, were being served to the elders. Leah's mouth watered. She loved them; though some people from "outside" the

Yukon turned their noses up at the thought of eating intestines. They didn't know what they were missing.

Lorna laughed.

"Don't expect any. Somebody knocked down a moose yesterday, there's only enough for the old folks at these do's."

The Ganaxteidi and other Raven clan members wove between the tables, feeding the elders first, the kids running and laughing – these were all her family. She felt a deep sense of contentment not felt for a long, long time. Lorna smiled: "It's good to have you here, Leah. You should move back home."

Haywire settled in on one of the side benches. It felt odd to Leah that he wasn't with her. With a knowing smirk, he watched his wife make her way toward the head table. His eyes met Leah's and the smirk was replaced by his gentle boy smile. Haywire's wife placed plates in front of Leah and Lorna.

"Here you go." she said. Leah and Lorna looked at each other, incredulous. "Did Lorraine actually just speak to you?" Lorna asked in a hushed voice.

"Where is my cell phone? Gotta call CBC radio." They both shook with laughter. That good feeling from the belly laugh.

They tucked into full bowls of soup and wild meat. Leah savoured each bite of wild meat, each drop of soup, as more and more food was placed in front of her. She knew protocol well enough not to refuse a thing. She knew she was to take anything she couldn't eat with her when she left and give it to a Raven family member. They must be famished, surrounded by all this good wild food. Dessert arrived. Moss berries fried in lard with sugar, Indian ice cream, pink and frothy and slightly bittersweet, cakes and pies.

"Oh, oh," she said to Lorna.

"What, oh oh?"

"I ate too much Indian ice cream and it is foaming up in my belly."

"Bloated belly is good. Haywire always did like you with meat on your bones." Lorna giggled breathlessly. Leah always overdid Indian ice cream. She adored the bittersweet tang.

The Speaker called Leah's name. It was time for her to sing. She rose and walked to the microphone with her guitar in hand.

She stood unspeaking for a moment and looked out across the gathering.

"My name is Leah Red Sky. My mother is Salteaux, and my father was Haudenosaunee and Salish, and Anishinabe. I am also Scots, English, and Spanish way back someplace." She heard people chuckling. She knew it was a loving unspoken teasing.

"I am a proud adopted member of the Daklaweidi Wolf Clan, through the Charlie family. I am very honoured to be in your traditional territory.

"I have been asked by the family to share a song. It's called 'Courage in My Eyes.' I wrote it for Angus."

The room was silent. Her eyes were closed. Her voice came like a creek, then a rushing powerful river. Haunting. Nuances of yearning: regret, longing for reunion. The fingers that plucked the strings of her guitar spoke of deep love. It was lyrical, repetitive, hypnotic.

෯

COURAGE IN MY EYES

Thunder rolling
all across
a crazy sky

star-fires burning
across the
ink blue night
one for
each of us
I know this
but I don't know why
I am flying
in an ink-blue sky,
with chips of fire
some people call stars
and there are no walls
and there are no barriers,
and I am free
I want to be a warrior
with courage in my eyes
I want to be a warrior
with courage in my eyes
And I will be
a warrior
with courage
in my eyes.

ॐ

Leah held silence at the end, as still as prayer. Opening her eyes, she smiled at the Charlie family and walked back to the table, the family members mouthed thanks as she passed. Lorna gave her a one-armed hug.

Dale Post swaggered with a long cowboy stride to the front. and the Speaker introduced him:

"The RCMP is taking over. Dale Post is going to make an event announcement."

Leah had never seen an event announcement at a funeral potlatch.

There was snickering. No one missed the little RCMP jab. Post did not introduce himself or say where he was from.

Not good, Leah thought to herself. The elders would want to know who his people were. This was very bad manners.

"I want to advertise an upcoming Native comedy event that you will all enjoy. It will be at the Kwanlan Din Cultural Centre in Whitehorse this Saturday at 7 o'clock p.m."

Lorna winced at the mispronunciation of "Kwanlin Dün." He name-dropped nationally known Indigenous comics. Leah leaned in to hear Lorna: "May be prettier than me, but he sure is full of himself." Lorna giggled.

"I wanted to say that the young lady that just sang would be a good person to go to a bar with." He feigned boxing. Someone in the crowd tittered.

"If she got into a fight, and there were Tlingits there, they would defend her. If there were Scottish people, they would defend her. English people would defend her…" Leah began to shake with anger. This was beyond teasing. He had some of the crowd laughing. She walked out of the Hall. Outside, she breathed in the cool air.

How dare he make fun of a respectful traditional introduction? Four young village men came out, nodded as they passed, walked down the steps and lit smokes. She heard a voice behind her.

"Gonna come and check out my comedy, fine white woman?"

Leah circled, facing him as he moved onto the lower steps. The men blew clouds of smoke, half-turned away, trying to be discreet.

"Our people," she began, "are so beautiful, so talented, so gifted. And then…" – she paused, he waited, smiling, intent – "there's *assholes* like you." His wide smile faded to an angry scowl. The men sniggered, one grinned, saying just loud enough to be heard: "Burn, baby, burn!"

Dale Post stomped across snow-covered gravel to a bright red truck and gunned the engine a little too hard, spinning icy gravel on the way out of the parking lot. The men raised their arms, in mock defence. Leah took a deep breath. Harry Peter smiled at her, winked as he said, "Good to have you back again, Wolf Sister."

Her anger was replaced by love. These people, their gentle way of edging you back into the circle, it was something she had missed. She walked back to the Hall just as a she saw five small boys standing in a circle at the front, obviously excited. The Hall thundered with drums as the little ones began to dance like wolves, howls possessing them. Leah's heart rose with the pride that was palpable in the room. If only time could stop, and she could stay within the beauty of this moment forever.

♋

Coyote is ravenous as he catches a scent on the wind. Spies a huge animal. Attacks. He cannot easily find the neck. He leaps, sinks his teeth into the flank. The cow moose bellows and bucks, Coyote holds on. The moose swings and stamps, turns this way then that to try to loosen the flinging thing that clings, whacks against her side. She bucks and sways, finally smashing the beast against a tree. Coyote, wind knocked out, lets go, stomach growling hard at the taste of blood in his mouth. The cow bolts off, left back flank bleeding. Coyote watches her go, licks blood off his lips and, when he recovers his breath, trots off hunkered low, tail down.

☙

FIRE AND ICE

I will say your name like a mantra
On my solitary journey through all the worlds
You always run from your shadow
The trouble is that's the part of you I love
I am like the girl who sees pictures in front of her eyes
To block out a world too cruel and I think that little girl is wise
I never wanted to own you, no, I just wanted to grow old with you
With you
It's always about saying goodbye, it's always about love and courage
We are like fire and ice – you burn, I melt
You burn, I melt, you burn, and I melt into nothing
Into nothingness itself
It's about justice it's about truth
There is a poverty of soul within me
All I'm left with is your name
And I will say your name
And I will say your name
And I will say your name like a mantra
On my solitary journey through all the worlds

CHAPTER SEVEN

As the plane rose to the sky, she had the feeling she was being pinned to her seat by the pressure.

Haywire had not come to see her off. But looking below as the aircraft circled, she spotted his truck idling in the parking lot, a heat cloud from the exhaust pipe. He had come to say goodbye in the only way he could. Leaving Haywire behind for the second time felt like an amputation.

❧

Leah blinked the damp from her eyes and focused on a sapphire-blue sky paling to aquamarine melting into opal clouds washed pink and gold from a setting sun. A river valley spirit snaked along black waters. Winter-white mist hung above slate mountains and deep valleys thick with snow. She watched until the dusk swallowed the sky colours. Finally, the coast appeared. Blue-black land, palest blue water at the horizon, like a watercolour. She did not feel ready. At all.

❧

ME AND NO ONE IN THE RAIN

Feeling young and small
beneath the city towers

Water running down my back
and making me shiver
Feel lost although
I know just where I'm going
It's okay to be lonely when you're alone
But to feel it with the one you love
That's really alone
Me and no one in the rain
Me and no one in the rain
This isn't how it was supposed to be
It wasn't how I planned it
It wasn't how it was supposed to be
Wasn't how I planned it
Isn't how I planned it

CHAPTER EIGHT

Leah put down the old diary. What was wrong with her? Her head hurt. She did not understand why she could not recall owning this or having written the words in the fat, moose-hide covered book stained with what looked like raindrops. Running a finger over the beadwork, she smiled, knowing this was Gramma Maisey's design. Wild roses. She imagined Gramma's tiny hands beading the piece, by candlelight or hissing lantern. It warmed her. She took a breath and thumbed through.

Her journal. Haywire had insisted. She trusted him. They had lived through too much together for her not to. It was undeniably her little sketches, her tiny script. She must have liked colour; there was every shade of ink.

At twenty-one, she had felt the need to create a life independent of her family. She moved thousands of miles north to Faro, a new mining town. It had been both exciting and terrifying. She remembered clearly the first time she'd driven in to Faro. The daunting hairpin turn took her breath with its sheer cliffs on either side just before the town site. A terrible wildfire had devastated the newly built town in the bush. Left a wasteland of burned-out wilderness, no trees. Low bush and purple fireweed showing through blackened, branchless trunks and stumps. Cypress Anvil Mine had stubbornly rebuilt a modern grouping of buildings to house miners in this blighted scape.

Leah sighed hard, bit her lower lip, and began to read. No doubt the words were hers, yet something deep in her was afraid to know what was between the pages. Heart pounding, she felt light-headed as she read.

ᘉ

July 10, 1993

Dammit to hell. Lost my journal on the flight North. I know I will never see it again. All those memories, secrets I hoarded away. If I ask myself now which entry I valued the most, I don't know what the answer would be.

Good thing I always record my songs someplace else. Maybe that's why I memorize them. No matter what, they're in my head and I can't lose them! Sometimes I wish I could write and read the language of music. Now I know why people always ask me "Are you still playing music?" because right now I can't play. It's like something is stuck in my throat.

I got this new diary from this guy I met. Haywire. I know; what a name. But he says never judge an Indian by his nickname. He has kind eyes, and a smile like a little boy. He said he got this journal in a potlatch gifting. He doesn't like to read or write. Mission school, he says. His Gramma beaded it especially for him.

Beadwork is unique up here. I love it. Especially like the wild roses – I LOVE wild roses and can't stop looking at the front of this thing!

I met Haywire after I got here. He works for the mine. I came up because I wanted to try a summer here. Vancouver didn't feel like home anymore. Next thing I know there's all these guys chasing me here. How did I know that there was two or three guys to every girl in a mining town? I was walking home from the post office, and guys kept slowing in their trucks and staring like I was rare wildlife. This guy walks up beside me, doesn't say anything, and just starts walking with me. I figure he's a deaf mute or something. He doesn't feel scary or anything, so I am good with it.

It turns out he knows where I live, which surprises me. He takes me right to the door of the trailer. Then walks off without saying anything. I asked my landlady about him. She says he don't talk much, but if he does, listen. Says he's interesting.

So, he keeps doing this walking beside me thing. Every day, after he gets off the mine shuttle. It makes the guys in the trucks quit slowing. The fourth time I say, "Hey – who says you can walk me home?" He just smiles. He says, "Well, those looks of yours and the few women in this town might just get you into some trouble!" He had a point. He just keeps walking me home, and then we become friends. He takes me in the bush around this place, shows me all kinds of things I haven't seen. The landlady was right. When he talks, I can learn a LOT. So, I just listen. That's a switch hahahaha. I haven't been called Motor Mouth and Magpie for nothing!

☙

Leah stopped reading. Her heart pounding, tears pushing at the backs of her eyes. She remembered these moments. But why did she not remember this journal? *It is my writing and I know that, but how could I not recall receiving it, owning it, or writing in it?* She turned the page.

☙

July 14, 1993
Haywire asked me to go to the dance at the Hall of the Rec Centre on Friday. I can't tell if it's as friends, or if he likes me. He's different from any other guy I've been around. I just want to be around him more.

Can't get enough of the bush walks. The other night we just sat there listening to the Moody Blues beside a lake. It was pretty weird to be out at midnight with the sun still out. I don't get tired with the midnight sun.

Haywire didn't make a move on me, but I caught him looking at me like he was trying to really perceive who I am. It kind of spooks me, because I don't feel him looking at me, and yet I kind of like it that he is. I guess I should decide if I want this thing to go further, because I have the feeling he wants to take it there.

July 20, 1993

Jesus, I did something really stupid. God, when I drink I do the stupidest things! Haywire and I were having beer at the dance. All kinds of guys wanted me to dance with them, and I said yes to be polite. Haywire watched me dancing, never asked anyone, but the women were asking him! I didn't see him dance once.

One guy, Mark, said, "I think your friend is jealous." I said, "I don't think so." He says, "Why else does he give me the look of death every time he catches my eye and you aren't looking?" I just laughed, but I wondered. About 10:00, Haywire said, "Let's get out of here." We ended up out at the lake. Nobody was around. I kissed him. Oh my God, what was I thinking? I effin' KISSED the guy! I should know by now never drink and never kiss. Because the next thing you know we were right into it. But he stopped right away when I asked him to. He wasn't mad, but I felt stupid. I just said, "I'm not really like this," and he nodded. I think I really like him. Any other guy wouldn't stop, would have been mad. We just stayed there and listened to the Moody Blues again for a couple hours. And then he drove me home. I hugged him, and he smiled that little boy smile that melts me. I want to see him already, and it's only five hours later!

Leah let the book fall into her lap. She recalled the fire between herself and Haywire. She'd felt it once again only days ago. She blushed. Why had she left him, and why in God's name had he let her go? Clearly there was something between them still. And why was it that could she not remember their breakup?

❦

July 21, 1993

I am with Haywire now. I love him. He doesn't say the "L" word, but I know he loves me too. I see it in his eyes, feel it when he touches me. I'm not gonna go fast though. I want to know we are good together before it goes further. Marriage does that. Makes you scared to try again. He doesn't push me about intimacy. He's respectful when I say, "No, I'm not ready yet." I told him I have to know we can get along well. He is okay with that, I guess, didn't say any different.

He says he wants to take me out to the bush for a couple of weeks. I'm really wanting to go, but I just got a job painting houses. It's like painting the same house over and over in a mining town.

❦

She remembered so well the deep feelings she'd had for Haywire, the passion, the conflict. It was alive within her now once more, as she relived each moment through her words. She had loved him so very much. She still did. God. Now, what the actual hell was she supposed to do?

❦

July 30, 1993

We've been out up the North Canol Road now for a week. I didn't write in here because we were busy getting ready and setting up camp. We got here via Ross River, this tiny little village. We got supplies there and took a little ferry across the Pelly River. The road itself was built by the U.S. Army during the Second World War. They came up to build a gas pipeline right to Norman Wells to secure a fuel supply.

One of Haywire's relatives was the one who went ahead of the Cats at Macmillan Pass. Grinding with their blades everything in their path to create what would be the road. I can't imagine the heavy equipment going through that country in the winter, tearing up the land.

I can't believe we're here! This is like when I was a kid and used to camp for whole summers. No, it's more than that. It's absolutely quiet here. The wild frightens me a little. I can feel the power of it. The mountains, the land. The road is one vehicle wide. We have seen nobody. It's the most beautiful place I've ever seen. This is the first truly wild place I've ever been.

The Macmillan Pass, at the top of the road, is just before the Northwest Territories border. It is a huge valley, with enormous mountains on either side that. rise out of the moose pastures at the side of the road. The moose pastures are huge sort of pristine swamps. The moose stand knee-deep and eat whatever plants grow there. The little hills are covered in moss berries. They look like blueberries, but are almost black, and are much tinier. They grow on fern-like plants flat against the ground and are the easiest things to pick ever. They are delicious. We found an outcropping of shale, and Haywire bashed a piece this way and that, and handed it to me after twenty or so minutes. He said, "Here, a tool to tan animal hides."

The wide expanse of this terrain has me feeling as free and connected to all things I've ever felt. I am part of all of this. Here, the past does not haunt me. The future does not tease. I am living completely in real time. Only here, there's the silence. For the first time in my life, I am deeply present. Still within.

He asked me to go home with him this winter and trap at Little Annie Lake. I couldn't say no. We're going to have a trapline! This has been my dream, to live rough! To live traditionally. I'm so excited! I need to prove to myself that I can do it. I never felt that Native, but out here it's like something has come alive in me. I hear, see, feel totally differently. I smell the wind like an animal. Listen deeply, I sense things.

This place is spectacular, wild and untouched except for the narrow gravel road, which is littered with old army trucks. Apparently, during construction of the road, if anything broke down it was simply buried or left and a new one was brought in. There are rusting, rotting forty-five-gallon drums here and there.

Yesterday we drove up to Macmillan Pass, and we saw a grizzly – my first! He was huge! Haywire just slowly turned the car and said, "We are just gonna leave you alone now Cousin, sorry to bother you!" He says bears can understand us. It sure seemed like it. That bear stopped and looked at us, stood up on hind legs like a man. It was like he was checking to see if we were really going to go!

Haywire was quiet for a while. Then he told me that when you meet a bear, you have to talk to it, because they are our cousins. You have to tell them why you're there, you're sorry you bothered them, and you're going to go. I was surprised he wouldn't just shoot first. I've watched too many movies.

I saw pictures in the "Whitehorse Star" of a car that was charged by a griz. It was peeled like a can of sardines. There's a mauling every year. I'm not scared up here, I know Haywire's a good shot. I saw it when he got grouse.

I love this place; the Pass is like being in a "National Geographic" magazine. The air is pure, you can drink from any creek, lake or river, and it's magnificent.

44

Leah closed her eyes for a moment and conjured the raw beauty
of the North Canol Road and the Macmillan Pass, the fragrance
of waking on spruce boughs, in what was known as a traditional
"brush tent." She and Haywire had made it together. She recalled
chopping up the earth and inserting the branches at an angle into
mossy soil. Nothing could replace standing still in the vast valley, with no sound but the breeze whispering in your ears.

❦

*Macmillan Pass itself, surrounded by the Mackenzie Mountains, is
astonishingly beautiful. As I said before, the pass is an enormous valley
a couple of miles wide, with mountains rising on either side of it. The
road cuts right through the middle. It's barely wide enough for two cars.
Bridges are only wide enough for one, which has made for some hairy
encounters when someone refuses to wait on the other side. There's a
ridiculous amount of wildlife out here. We've encountered a few hunters,
but for the most part people leave you alone.*

I've been dreaming a lot out here, maybe because my mind is quiet.

*We stopped in at the little camp we saw up in the Pass. It was two
Indian women our age from Ross River! I couldn't believe how they could
comfortably camp so close to a grizzly. They had a couple of kids, one
about four, a baby, and one just able to walk. I asked Haywire how the
heck they keep them so quiet. The only way I knew someone was in that
camp before we walked in was because there was smoke coming out of the
wall-tent stovepipe. Haywire says they teach newborns how to be quiet
and the kids just learn. They don't say a word when they see you walk
in, just stare at you. The women were really quiet too, but they offered
us food and tea.*

I love the campfire tea. They pick what they call "bush tea" and brew it up with fresh spring water. It's good medicine. It's all we've been drinking after our store-bought ran out. I love the stuff.

The wall tent is thrown over a tent frame. Frames are all over the place out on the land. When people make them, they leave them behind for others. It's the way of the people here.

❧

Bush tea. The little bag Haywire had gifted her with at the end of the potlatch. The waxy leaves were redolent of wild places and mountains. Leah brewed a big pot, anticipating the lightly smoky taste. She settled back on the white couch, blowing on a steaming cup of amber liquid, releasing the fragrance of the land she loved. She closed her eyes. Memories were kindled and fanned.

❧

Haywire says how they keep babies quiet is to give them a chunk of moose fat to suck on to keep them from getting hungry. (Note: they tied the chunk to string attached to the baby's foot. When and if the baby choked, it would kick and pull out the fat). That and they have moss bags, so when they mess themselves, they don't feel uncomfortable. I asked about bugs in the moss (I was wondering if I could use it for my time). I asked one of the ladies and she told me the secret. To use smoke from a fire to release any insects. So, I can use it if I need to. I'm running out of stuff for my time – geez, I better learn how to plan better, I thought we'd go into Ross to pick up what we need by now. Maybe it's time to ask Haywire. I've been thinking how much I want a baby with him.

Haywire is different. He's happy and peaceful out here. This is how he loves to live.

❧

DANCE AWAY, Verse 5

You spoke of spring-blossomed tree
and one gust of wind
causing it to sacrifice
petals of palest pink
Are you asking me
to be like this tree?
Oh please, please
do not ask this of me
Better that I dance away.

❧

In the cold light of morning, Leah thinks perhaps she should begin a new journal. It could help to remember what she has lost of herself. Another thought comes, and it chills her: What if she has a form of dementia and starts forgetting the new journal? This brings up a sick feeling. The old diary pulls at her. She does not want to read the words, yet they lure her.

❧

POETRY IN THE CASTING

I have a longing this morning
to hear your laugh, your voice, or see your smile
so I am writing a few lines; casting out a line.
Doesn't matter if I catch anything,

there is poetry in the casting
and I'm learning a lot about that of late.

I am still deep in the throes of learning
exploring my caves
with no light
and no way of knowing
what I might find there
And there is art everywhere
I'm learning to fill my soul, fill my soul

❧

August 20, 1993

Went to town and we ran into a bunch of Haywire's cousins. They made a big deal out of Haywire having a girlfriend. They're all very handsome, and all different. Johnnie is a flirt, with high cheekbones, a grin that doesn't go away, and his laugh reminds me of a little kid. He likes to joke a lot. Joe, his brother, couldn't be more different. Shy, serious, and quiet. Sammy is from another family and has beautiful white teeth. He is always smiling too but is like a big kid. Nolan, Sammy's brother, is more quiet like Joe. They all look like they would be a little wild if they started partying, though.

Most of them play music. We sat around and swapped songs. They drop beats, which is strange, but must be the way they hear the music. It was fun to meet them. None of them talk about girlfriends. They teased me like a sister, and I fell in love with every last one of them.

Haywire and I have been at Little Annie at his Mom's for a week now. He gets a week off for every four weeks on. I gave up trying to get work in town.

His mom cried when she first saw him. I think they must have fought last time they saw each other, because she said, "Sonny, sonny, I didn't think you'd come back," and hung onto him for a long time. It was likely about me. She hasn't liked me from the word "go." He's getting pissed off about it. Last night, she wouldn't sit with us at the table for dinner. He asked her why she wasn't sitting with us, and she made some excuse about being too hot. That didn't wash – she was sitting closer to the barrel heater. She moved to the table but didn't look happy. She ignores me for the most part. The only thing she says is, "Can you make fire? Are you gonna be able to run fish nets with bare hands in the winter?" When I always say yes, she just looks at me like there is no way I can do either. I will prove her wrong if it kills me.

I met Uncle Angus. He came down the morning after we got here. How he knew we were here I have no idea. He packed a whole caribou quarter down for us!

҂

A winter of caribou steaks and eggs for breakfast, that quarter hung in the frigid porch all winter long. Leah's stomach tightened, thinking of the delicious aroma and taste of fresh caribou steaks. Her mouth watered, and she went to get a chunk of dry moose meat from the kitchen. It wasn't caribou, but it had the taste of smoke and the wild.

҂

I know the caribou wasn't for Doris. For some reason, Angus and Doris don't get along, that's what Haywire said. Her house has a closed-in porch out front, and it's already cold enough in there to hang meat. So, when you walk in from outside, there's the quarter hanging there.

49

Rustic. We've been sawing off steaks for breakfast and supper. My new favourite breakfast is caribou steaks and eggs. It is so good! Succulent, full of wild flavour. I don't have to eat again until supper! But I have been told that a person should not live on caribou alone.

Uncle seems to really love Haywire; they had a lot of catching up to do over tea. Well, Haywire did. Uncle Angus listens. With a "maybe, too" or "uh huh" here and there. I like him a lot. He doesn't look or act like Doris (thank God!) – and geez, I better hide this journal – but the way she talks I don't think she can read (hahahaha).

Uncle is a small, wiry old guy. He has the sweetest smile I have ever seen (well, besides Haywire's). When we were introduced, he was shy, but I saw the most kindness I have ever seen in any man's eyes. I wanted so much to hug him, but he is old-fashioned, so I knew not to. One day I will, though.

ᴖ

Doris's house was an old army shack, a remnant from the era of the Second World War. From when the American Army came through to build the Alaska Highway. Leah guessed those green-horns back then didn't have the sense to insulate it. The only heat was from heater made from a rusty old forty-five-gallon barrel with a metal plate welded to the top. When you first walked in, there had been an enclosed porch. Right inside the front door a washstand. To the left there was a kitchen counter with a propane stove and a small bathroom sink that drained into a bucket.

Doris kept that stove immaculate. On the barrel heater was a perpetual kettle of hot water. If there was no propane that barrel heater top was used for cooking.

The bedrooms had a space left open between the ceiling and the walls, so the heat could come through. It didn't. She laughed thinking about herself and Haywire squeezing together in his single bed.

Leah had desperately missed running water. At Doris's there wasn't any for a couple of miles. They mostly melted snow in the cold weather. She shuddered, remembering that if she was up last, she was expected to wash in the water that Doris, Haywire and his sister had used. It was a revolting grey.

Their diet, besides the caribou, had been sparse. Fried potatoes for breakfast, macaroni for lunch with canned meat or tomatoes, and fried baloney, or just canned tomatoes. The leftovers for supper. Doris made fantastic bread, though.

When Leah and Haywire went out with the .22 they came back with grouse, and rabbits. She couldn't get enough of the wild food.

Hauling water was a constant pain. It involved a several-mile walk along the road if the truck broke down or ran out of gas, which happened often. Doris hated carrying the buckets from the closest stream and ran off the road into the bush every time a car came. She said she hated it when the white people stared as they passed. Leah hadn't seen a white person yet, just Indians going by. She would drop her bucket and hide, too. Her arm needed a break, and the buckets were dead heavy.

☙

August 26, 1993
Haywire went up to visit his Aunt Laylie, and he told me she said, "Hey, bring that Kutchen up here so I can get a look at her!" I guess they heard I was light-skinned, so they think I'm white.

I hope the rest of the family likes me better than Doris does.

September 1, 1993

I can't believe Haywire's cousins Sammy and Johnnie came all the way out here to Little Annie from Whitehorse. Just to tell me there are going to be open auditions for the big music festival in Faro. They aren't interested, because it's folk music. They're all about country rock. I know I have a shot, but I haven't been playing for a while so I'm probably pretty rusty.

September 2, 1993

I'm on my way to the audition in Whitehorse. I'll start practising again right here in the truck after I'm done trying to write this (which is why this is so messy!) I'm going to play "Your Cheatin' Heart," and two of my songs, not sure which yet. I used to hate Hank Williams, but since I've been listening to only him on the truck cassette player, I've been indoctrinated into the Church of Hank Williams. His lyrics are like deep water: there are exquisite layers down into the cold deep.

September 2, later

I got in! Sammy and Johnnie were really cute. When we got there, they acted like security and stood with their arms crossed. I don't know where they got the sunglasses. They were ridiculous and adorable. It was hard not to burst out laughing.

As soon as I started to sing, they busted out in their usual crazy grins. Sammy was snapping his fingers and tapping his feet, and Johnnie was mouthing all the words. I guess he listened more than I ever thought. They didn't notice that I didn't drop beats all over the place like them. I figure it has to do with the traditional rhythm in their blood. Sammy and his brother both do it, and I figure it's the ancient rhythm of this land. It sounds and feels right to them, and to me.

I'm so excited! I am playing in my first big International festival! And I found out at the audition that it will be fed live over CBC across

Canada! People everywhere will hear me! This might be my big break. I would so love to play music for a living.

Those who don't write have no idea how much it takes to create a song. I remember sitting in my sister's kitchen in North Van. I was writing "Seasmoke" and sat playing the first two lines over and over. In the sun on the back-door sill. It had probably been an hour of me repeating, repeating. Sis was puttering around in her kitchen, and in her usual patient and kind way, she said, "Can you play something else for a while?" That was the first time I really understood the work involved with writing a song, and how much practise it takes, line by line. Before, just did it.

☙

Leah looked out at the North Shore Mountains across the water from downtown Vancouver. She heard the front door of the condo close and called to Phillip:

"You're home late."

"Yeah. Bill had something he needed to talk to me about. He's is pretty depressed."

"Is that because his name is actually Adele?" she said under her breath. It was clear their relationship was in its death throes but neither of them seemed to want to pull the plug on it.

"I'm just going to take a shower."

Sure. Because drinking in a sports bar with "Bill" is such a sweaty activity. Ass. She went back to the journal.

☙

I also got how it drives other people crazy when you repeat a couple of lines of a developing song over and over and over. After that, I tried to do it in private. People are only interested in hearing finished songs. Other than songwriters, that is. Songwriters love to hear partial songs; they get to hear the possibility when you stop after one verse and chorus. And no matter where the song stops, even after a verse, they are enthralled, and can't wait to hear the whole thing.

Oh my God, I can't believe next month. I can hardly wait! I'm going to practise my ass off. Nobody will know the length of their sets, or how many. Until you get a program when you get there. Oh yeah – and there are workshops we're expected to be in, too. That's a little nerve-racking. I can't prepare for a workshop when I don't know the theme. I guess they're trying to create some magic, but wow, talk about putting pressure on the performers! I can do this! I will do this! This is my dream coming true.

September 3, 1993
Haywire is jealous. I've never seen this before. I was so excited to get back and tell him about the festival, but all he did was look at me and walk out of the house. He went down to the lake, I guess, because he's been gone for a long time. Doris didn't say much, but Uncle was really happy for me. I explained about festivals, since I don't think he would have been to one. He said, "You got good songs; it's good people gonna hear 'em." I will play the one I wrote for him ("Courage in My Eyes") and dedicate it to him; but I won't tell him until the performance, and then I'll surprise him! I'm sad about Haywire. I really expected him to be happy for me. He is absolutely not.

☙

Leah stopped reading, on a whim grabbed her phone. Dialled.

"Haywire?"

"That would still be me." Leah could hear the happiness in his voice as he recognized hers.

"Haywire, what the hell went wrong with us?"

Deep silence.

"Leah, it's…complicated. I think…we were young. Things were just harder than we knew how to get through them."

"It makes me wonder. There was nothing I remember that was enough to split us up. I remember you drinking near the end, I remember you being mad at me quite a bit, but we loved each other so much – why didn't we work it out?"

"Leah, let's talk about it…next time you're up."

"I just feel so sad, Haywire. I'm reading that old diary, and it brings up all my feelings for you. How deep they were – are. My relationship with the white guy I told you about is a hot mess. It's all making me think you and I should have stuck it out."

He fell quiet for so long she thought the connection might have been lost. But she knew this silence and waited.

"Leah, know that I love you, and always will. Sometimes life…just…gets in the way."

"Well, we shouldn't have let it."

"Chaos…"

She could hear in the name and within his silence the words he could not speak.

♧

September 10, 1993
Haywire finally told me what's bugging him. He says he's afraid I will leave. As he puts it, I'm as good as anyone on the radio. He's afraid I'll have to move to the city to have a career. He says he'll never live in a city, because Whitehorse is bad enough. He has seen cities on TV and in movies, and he knows he would hate them. He is wrong. I would stay wherever he is and travel as needed from there.

I'm sad: I always thought he would come with me. Be offstage smiling at me when I played. I guess that fantasy of mine is just that. How could I leave him here and go? My heart would break! He says he knows other men will want to be with me. I tell him he is the only man I want. He just shakes his head.

How could this be the way it is? My dream is coming true and I have no room to be happy about it! I cry when I'm splitting wood, so nobody sees. But that's dangerous, I'm likely to hit myself with the axe. I better cry when we haul water and walk behind Doris, so she won't see.

ℚ♪

In her new journal, Leah writes: Today, I am free. Or am I? I will still sit inside this cage, and for a long while will not remember that the door has been opened. My mind is still in the prison. Gradually, I will understand that I am not. The crow is nagging at someone else now. I'm like a rescue cat. I'll be skittish and unsure, I expect. In a dream, Haywire asked for an important keepsake and I said, "But I don't remember" and began to wonder what else I've lost of my life – I realized in the dream that I was having blackouts. This was a terrible thought.

"Don't worry," says the woodpecker. "He wishes for you to doubt; it gives him power as you are distracted from your own." It's Phil the woodpecker is speaking of. Moon Power is what I own today. "Yes," says the woodpecker, who has moved closer. A lone goose calls. I do not listen. The woodpecker says, "It's nothing" from a distance again. A seagull cries: "Lonely, lonely."

Humans are intruding now nearby. "Humph," says the goose. I will listen well to the creatures today; speak gently. Well, except for the goose, who is a little judgemental.

All my life I've longed to comprehend to converse with the geese, otters, gulls, and squirrels. "Oh, have you?" mutters a squirrel, who runs erratically, arrogantly around the garden like he owns it. I call him Bart. He staccato-chatters now at the gulls, telling them to keep their distance. He tears up trees, leaps from one delicate branch to another leaving them swaying wildly behind him. A bird now asks, "When, when, when, when?" And I answer, "NOW!"

But still I will hide this journal from Phil, who would make fun of it. No, I will NOT. Not now! If I do hide this, I am closing my OWN cage door. "Oh!" hollers the crow, nearby. Four geese cross, close, west to east. Thank you, grandmothers. "Thanks, thanks, thanks, thanks," affirms crow. I ignore the seagull, who has nothing good to say but shrieks like an old woman. Neurotic. Crossing east to west, the geese seem confused, unsure. I choose to walk, determined in ONE direction: HOME. To myself.

♡

ME AND NO ONE IN THE RAIN, *Verse Three*

It's a long, long way from the wooded hills
And the quiet people
It's a long, long way from the wooded hills
And the quiet water, quiet water
Me and no one in the rain
Me and no one in the rain

This is the place of the body but not the heart
Should have known it better from the start
This is the place of the body but not the heart
I should have known it better from the very start
Me and no one in the rain, oh
Me and no one in the rain

October 29, 1993

The sea is restless, pale grey. The sky an ocean above, ready to come down again as rain. The trees fuss, each leaf nervous, waiting. A crow races across, west to east. There are no creatures speaking. None to be seen. The hummingbird feeder hangs, swaying to and fro, to and fro, to and fro. My heart is stone. Heavy, cold, old. It does not move within me or feel. It's like a cold fire pit. My heart's fire is stone, deep cold.

Last night it happened again – spirits are coming one by one in dreams and telling their stories. I don't want to remember. If I don't write them down, they say they will keep coming to me. I am crazy. I will never tell anyone this. I can't even bear how they might look at me. I can't look at myself!

POETRY IN THE CASTING

I have a longing tonight
to be heard to be seen
to be known and understood
Not to have to explain
and justify
and I cannot help but wonder
where are you, my friend
Are you alone tonight,
alone with somebody
alone and content
or lonely with somebody
or just alone

CHAPTER NINE

"Haywire?"

"Chaos, what's wrong?"

"Haywire, I need to know something." Silence.

"What?"

"Haywire, did you leave me because I was a bitch?"

"Hardly. You left me 'cause I was an asshole."

"Haywire…you know me better than anyone ever did." Silence. His voice was very soft.

"I say the same about you all the time."

"To who?"

"Uncle."

She cried now, wailing like a child. Haywire's silence fell, heavy.

"Oh God, Haywire, I miss Uncle… my life is a mess."

"Welcome to the club, Leah, everyone's is."

"Phillip just took off to be with his white woman."

"Who is Phillip?"

"Very funny. I told you about him when I was there."

"I know, just tryin' to give your face a rest. Smile, it takes fewer muscles!"

"I can't be with Indian guys, I can't be with white guys."

"Me either."

Leah laughs bitterly through her tears at his silly attempt at humour. "Oh, my God, Haywire – you kill me!"

"Someone has to make you laugh, Leah."

"You always knew how to make me feel better." Silence.

"Not always, Leah."

"Haywire..."

"Chaos?"

"Thanks for listening, I'm going to go jump out the window now."

"That's good... Leave your guitar to me and say 'hi' to the seagulls on the way down."

"Bye."

"See ya."

She imagines he sits for a long time, smoking outside. The river is icing over, but he can still hear the water running underneath. That he can hear his kids inside, his wife moving dishes in the kitchen. She feels he will need to stay with thoughts of her for a while; will not have liked how she sounded. For the next four days, at dawn and sunset, he will go out; say her name to the wind. The wind will catch it and dance it all the way over across the river, beyond the forest, all the way to the meadows. The ravens will pick up the sound, hop, flap. They always hear. They will echo her name; while the meadow sits silent, waiting. Waiting for her.

❧

Thursday

I am by the water in the garden. I can't do anything but sit. Last night, a terrible storm within me; this morning, I survey the damage and wonder how can I pick up so many tiny splinters of my heart and my life's dreams to put them back together again? A new heart within is a large stone. Cold and darker grey than the sea this morning. The geese were speaking, and I did not listen. They crossed in a line east to west.

"Look!" one commanded. There were many, one by one in a long line. "Look!" What is it I'm supposed to see? Geese are most unwise. I do as they say,but I am not receiving the message they bring. I'm as unsettled as those shaking trees above me. Restless as the sea. Tears are swollen inside me and I feel as grey as the sky, ready to rain. A crow off in the distance. I cannot hear clearly what he says. No creature has anything to say today? This, then, is what hopelessness feels like? A gull goes back and forth. That crow, in the distance, speaks to another today. What is it that everything seems to be waiting for? Today I long to see the mountain that occasionally appears to the south; it is obscured, has been for weeks, perhaps months. If it was visible, I did not see it. Phil. I hated his behaviour in some ways. But something in me wishes it had worked. Why do things that start out so good end so badly?

Friday
I can't stay away from reading the diary. Or writing in this journal. In truth, both terrify me! Up late today. A robin said, "Your life, now." I opened the deck door to allow the morning air in. Now she says, "Beauty, beauty, beauty, beauty." The repeating bird insisting "Pray, pray, pray, pray." A crow: "Found, found." A raven! Very distant. "Go, go, go, go, and go." Where, grandfather? "Home." A crow: "Now, now, now." The insistent bird, "Sing, sing, sing, and sing…beautifully" the insistent bird is still advising me to pray. The geese spoke of love, to one another across the water. Echoing back and forth. The insistent one is saying, "Be, be, be" over and over. There is so much. It is a soft, gentle morning. Today my heart is floating in tears. I will allow my heart to be an ancient, ocean-going war canoe – readying for a journey. Salish people must wait for the weather to travel. We have patience in this. So, must I. "Excitement," thrills a young robin "See? See? Secret! Secret! See? See secret! See?" The insistent bird continues, "Pray and sing," over and over.

A cold gale blows through Vancouver. The fragrance of dead fallen leaves, diesel. The constant shush of tires on the wet. The roar and rattle of a busy construction site.

"Auntie! Auntie!" Leah stops, turns, confused. A rumpled, unwashed young Cree man, an innocent face hardened by a burden of suffering, holding something out to her. The diary.

"Auntie. The truth is inside you. But you need this. You *need* it." Leah can't speak. He nodded once, chin up – the way all Indians do. Wearing a genuine, open Indian grin, he held out the wet diary.

"You dropped it, Auntie. Don't give up. You'll remember. You're strong. You'll find your power, Auntie…be who you are."

And he is gone.

❧

Sunday
The insistent bird tells me, "Speak, speak, speak, speak, speak, speak." Yet another soft gentle day. The water rippled but peaceful. The trees barely move. The swan was by, east to west, quickly, which is not usual. What, my dear bird, is it that I am supposed to speak? To whom? "To your friend, there," says the young robin in his cheerful voice. He repeats. What friend? The homeless man? I will learn to speak the truth.

But this truth, that comes with fear, will not reveal itself to me!

❧

Leah flashed her pass at the security guard. Why was there heavy security at the Ministry? Every floor locked down. What were they expecting, terrorists?

The first day she had walked into Crown-Indigenous Relations and Northern Affairs – or "Treaties 'R' Us" as she jokingly called it – she had looked in vain for Native faces. It was a heart-sinking feeling, but one she learned to live with. Most Native folks moved on quickly. Why, Leah wondered, was *she* still there? The constant demands from the Minister's office were like dealing with a constantly sick, snotty-nosed, whiny kindergarten kid. She felt like 1-800-Dial-an-Indian. The time she had fifteen minutes to inform the Minister how to act in a smudging ceremony. Or how to pronounce a Salish word that was about a sentence long, filled with little glottal-stop sevens. Her response had been, "Your guess is as good as mine."

❧

Monday
Clearest blue sky. I don't understand the frantic gull. The water is almost perfectly calm. The trees are unmoving.

"Take, take," other gulls holler; "View, view, view." The gull has calmed now that I got the message. His friends echo. They speak quickly and consistently, like small barking dogs.

"Hurry, hurry, hurry," says the insistent bird.

Yesterday there were ravens. I could not understand those voices – but they are tricksters, so may not have wanted me to.

Finally, the seagulls have slowed their barking. I need rest, restoration. Clarity. Now it is important for me to figure out what it is that I need. A sit by quiet water, or the fragrance of old-growth forest? "Health, health," a gull yelps over and over.

I miss the robin – especially the joyous sound of the little one. And my insistent bird didn't stick around this morning. The water is perfectly still, now. I am not.

℘

Leah closed the door to her office, looked at the photos on her desk. The half-smile of Gramma Maisey. Haywire; and Uncle Angus, her late father, and her great-grandmother with her usual sweet, tired smile.

The first email was from the Minister's office, requesting a rush response for the usual inane information. Another request to submit her time card. Shit. She had missed the deadline. Again. She looked to the sky beyond her window. The skeletal leaf-bare trees. She longed to see buds. Signs of Spring.

℘

Wednesday
I hear a lone goose, but it's hard to understand. "Look, look, look, look." Water, trees, sky, all calm. The neighbour ladies stripped my garden. Placed bits of driftwood and pots in a beautiful way. "Girl Power," they said. They wanted to help because they know Phil left, and they thought I needed a lift, so they surprised me. I didn't tell them they had disrupted my planting of rare exotic bulbs. What they did is incredibly touching and lovely, though I liked the wild charm of my garden. Their love is far more beautiful! The unity of women lightens our hearts, eases our way. We forget the quiet, gentle strength we own. Our love, compassion, as delicate as a spider thread, can hold like steel cable. Drill deep like diamond. We grow a power even we do not understand.

I cannot stop crying for something I have lost. I wish I knew what.

To: *raymondtull@cbcnorth.ca*
From: *leah.growingthunder@shaw.ca*
Subject: *Request for Interview, CBC "North Musicians: Where Are They Now?" Project*

Hi Raymond,
I looked at your most recent list of questions and think it may be best if we do a phone interview. It is going to end up being a very slow process otherwise! I'll try my best to answer the questions you sent. I'm available after 6:30 any night. I look very much forward to speaking with you.
Leah

Friday
The rain is insistent today, determined, steady. The geese speak below, in the distance. I hope they speak of love.

The weather has rendered the world outside into an old oil painting. The softness of trees all around the water. Off, distant, the mountain stands guard somewhere through the mist. The mountains keep calling to me in dreams. Standing, watching, like sentient living beings. They know. Why do I not? In dreams every night, and just before I wake, I cry for something I have lost.

Chapter Ten

Thirsty, she got a glass of water. When the phone rang, she spilled water on her lap.

"Hello?"

"Hi, Leah, Ray. I think I would've recognized your voice anywhere. I've been listening to archived CBC North recordings. It's beautiful. Leah, you have a gorgeous voice, and your songwriting is breathtaking!"

"Thanks, Raymond."

"Ray."

"Okay, Ray. Call me Genius." (Leah heard delight in his voice. And his laugh felt like a reward she had earned).

"When you left for the Yukon, did you leave Vancouver behind?"

"It was a terrible situation that I needed to put behind me. I think when we have a sad life, it makes us good artists."

"Why did you stop performing?"

"Next question." (Something uncoiled in her belly).

"So, about sad beginnings and good artists?"

"There's a gift in every bad thing."

"How so?"

"Like a ring of fire – those trials of life. You have to get through it. You can run around in that ring of fire screaming about how much it hurts. Or, you can look for the gift that's hidden in the fire, grab it, and run out to the other side as fast as you can."

"Does that show up in your lyrics?"

"Listen to 'Fire Within.' The gifts are profound understandings of self, zendagi."

"Zendagi?"

"Sorry. It's Persian for 'life' – the conceptual meaning would be a paragraph in English."

"What other songs allude to this gift?"

"'Dance Away' is more about relationships, letting go. Same with 'Me and No One in the Rain,' and 'Fire and Ice.'"

"You must miss music, songwriting, performing?"

"It was like abandoning a child, but the chasm between you and the child seems insurmountable, because you can't forgive yourself."

"Sounds very painful."

"Not in the *least*. (He snorts). "Next question." (The uncoiled something slow-crawled in her belly) *No, not the intrusion of fog enshrouded memories. Why had she left Haywire, the North?*

"Would you consider a reunion festival here?"

"I...don't know." (The slow-crawler was coiling and recoiling).

"Why?"

"I don't know." (The slow-crawler; she jumped).

"Ever thought of getting help?"

Leah seethed. He heard her say through gritted teeth.

"Next question."

"Am I standing on a nerve again?"

"Yes, with your size fifteen hunting boot."

"Sorry. 'Fire Within' is hypnotic."

"Repeat, call and answer. It's a technique."

"Listen, Raymond – I have to go." (The slow-crawler had recoiled).

"Okay, Leah. Call again in a week?"

"Fine; but I really have to go."

Leah sat looking at her cell. Each silence between her words was a universe. She wanted to know and understand this silence that existed between her words.

❧

THE SAME ROAD

The secret in your eyes you've never told
Sometimes I see it and it shines like gold
We both know you and I have always walked the same road
You gave the gift of all your dreams
You taught me how to laugh, how strange it seems
That you'd cry now
I've held your dreams safe, come take them now

❧

Leah listens, eyes closed, to her song. As though this voice is not hers. Her singing from long ago. Chills roll up and down her. The voice caresses places deep in the chasms of her silences. Places within her that she has forgotten. It washes over her like cleansing water in a sacred purification rite.

❧

The winds of hell have grounded you
And mad dogs have surrounded you
Lost from home

68

And still you've grown
Standing all alone, all alone
Like birds in the dust we all are blind in heart
And the yellow winds of fate can tear our wings apart
Still we can fly
Up through the rain to the sky
The wild falcon's path we must fly
Don't you look behind
Your dreams are going to pass you by

The secret in your eyes you've never told
Sometimes I see it, it shines like gold
We both know
You and I will always walk the same road

☙

Conjuring within the subtle nuances of her voice. The song and old friends. She calls to her own spirit now. Calls her spirit home to herself. Yearning. The promise of new beginnings. She submits, again and again, to this calling. Still, she cannot answer.

☙

Leah watched Ray as he stood looking at the spectacular view from her living room. His CBC broadcaster voice did not match his appearance. She looked at his beautiful high cheekbones, and deep brown skin. The eyes that shone. The thick, long black hair. His candid look, typical of a Northern man. Something deep in her opened to him.

She watched as he walked about and picked up a delicately woven basket next to her. Small enough to sit in his palm, perfectly woven, with a lid that fit over top. He opened it. The coloured designs woven in had faded on the outside but were still bright inside. Dark green birds all around, red and black stripes underneath. On the lid, a circle in red, outlined in yellow and black like a sun. Around that swam five green geese. She'd always found it exquisite, whimsical.

Ray looked up when she said, "My grandmother made that. It's all I have of her."

He carefully replaced it on the small table.

"I wish I'd known her, but we were kept away." She heard the tone of her own voice. It sounded as if she was about to cry. "Come on, the food is ready. Dinner's Northern-style."

Ray took his first bite, closed his eyes.

"*Where* did you learn how to cook moose steaks so tender and delicious?"

"I'll be right back."

Returning, she handed him a black frame with an old black-and-white photograph.

"Uncle Angus." The old face, with the wide almost toothless smile, poised on a pushed over wringer washer. Hitching up his jacket at the back as the photo was snapped. She loved this photo of Uncle's open face. The face of a man who had nothing to hide. It looked as though he had just said something funny, had just laughed.

"What a wonderful smile."

"He was the real love of my life, the only man who loved me for who I was, with no expectations. He just seemed to enjoy me being around. I miss him."

"He's gone?"

"Not long ago. I'll never really get over it." Her voice was shaking. He wanted to remove the grief that seemed to have cloaked her. She felt tears choking her throat. He grabbed his glass of water and held it up."Cheers to the ancestors who invented bannock."

She looked at him and her throat opened a little as she laughed. She gave him that, he was trying.

"Cheers – you really are a Crow."

His smile was slow, sensuous. She wanted to kiss that smile right off him.

She said, "I'm Wolf, can you tell?" It was a test. They could not be together unless they were opposite clans.

His eyes lit up. Good. He was interested.

He was looking out the window. She could only focus on his lips and how they would feel. His tongue touching hers. Why was she thinking like this when she'd wanted to cry just a moment ago?

Her expression was one of invitation. Her full lips open, he could see that her breath was coming fast. Her head tipped back ever so slightly. He crossed to her and she watched him come. He reached out and grasped gently a handful of hair, pulling her face to his. She did not resist. They joined lips for slow, lingering kisses, no sound but their breath.

She gripped his bottom; he laughed quietly, his "yes." She popped his shirt buttons, they ding-ding-dinged all over the kitchen.

"Tomorrow we will buy you all snap-front shirts. Ten; that is, if I let you out of this house."

With a ripping of fabric, she tossed her dress aside. She had been wearing almost nothing underneath. Ray buried his face in her neck and inhaled her scent. Tasting one, then the other breast, tongue hot on her nipples. She moved backward to lean on the counter. He tore his jeans off. He lifted her to the countertop. She wanted, needed him inside, parted her legs wide. He plunged into her. She cried out, clinging to him. He pounded, and she felt him pulsing inside her just as she crested her wave.

He said, breathless, "Wait."

She was so filled with desire she could not wait. She kissed him deeply. She hopped down, turned to the counter with her bottom to him and pulled him to her. Her moans voice filled the room.

He was engorged, and she was deliberate as she turned, lowered to her knees and used her tongue, hands, breath on him. He shuddered as she then slowly, gently pushed him to the floor. She was on top of him, and he was ready, wanting. They were skin on skin. Leah cried out as he entered her. She bucked and writhed under him. She was tight, wet. It took everything in him to hold back.

She slipped out from under him, was on all fours, and looking back at him. He entered her. The angle of her insides against his penis made her moan out loud. She shifted her hips again, again. He grasped her breasts and she called out his name. She rolled on her back, pulled him to her, and raised her legs in the air. She held her breasts. His mouth and tongue hot on her nipples. He sucked the sweetness of her. They rolled as she climbed on him, and like a dancer, slow moved, rocking her pelvis so she could feel everything inside of her. She slowly lay down on him. Carefully turned until she was facing to the side, then away from him. It was unbearably sweet, moving so slowly, deliberately. He caressed her all over as she turned. He closed his eyes, while she revelled in the sensation of him deep within her – other-worldly; a deep erotic meditation.

They rested, slept. Without a word, he felt her move and opened his eyes. She climbed and straddled him until he was deep inside her. Deliberately, Leah felt him fill her the way she needed him to, rode him in a way that made his head touch every wall of her insides. She lunged herself back and forth on him. She felt a sudden sweet pang and she cried, loud and long with intense, sweet pleasure. Finally, she lowered herself to him, still holding him within her. They rested and spoke softly, sometimes silent. After a time, she began again. He hardened when she slowly swivelled her body sideways. She was taking him deep and slow, deep and slow. She leaned back, moaning. Then, furious, and fast, she brought herself home with a yowl. When she fell back he brought her cold water. She drank and then poured water from her mouth to his chest, bringing an ache to his groin. Then she took him in her cool mouth, bringing him to hardness again.

She kissed him slowly, exploring until she found his tongue. With her eyes on his, he moaned when she kneeled, taking him in. Her mouth hot on his skin. He lost himself in the sensation of the heat of her tongue. He moaned, keened, allowed himself to release, calling her name.

She trembled at his touch. The primal scent of sex filled the room. They said nothing as they rested and fell asleep entwined there on the floor.

꘎

The two of them in a restaurant on a mountainside in West Vancouver. All cedar, West surrounded in West Coast Native art. The view spectacular. The lights on the distant ships were framed by the lights of Spanish Banks, Musqueam First Nation, the University Endowment Lands.

Leah opened an ache in Ray's chest as he looked at her intently, instead of at the places she pointed out in the distance.

"Tell me how you were as a child."

"Ray, it's a sad story. It'll be hard for me to tell. Maybe this will help me to remember some things."

She took a deep breath and let it out slowly.

"I grew up thinking I was white, in white neighbourhoods. All-white grade schools. But knowing I was very different. I didn't learn the same way. See things the same way.

"Years later, I came home from high school one day After learning about what happened to Indian people. I had seen the play *Bury My Heart at Wounded Knee*. Every kid in that high-school play was white. Not one Indian acted in that play.

"I was possessed by the story. The awful naked truth of it. It enraged my being. I took my outrage home to my father. He got really, really still." He said, "I will tell you this because you are showing respect. We are Indian. You are Indian." That hit me like a fist in my belly.

"I knew the truth of it in every cell of my body. *I am Indian*. And for years, that reality lay as still as my father; waiting."

Leah was momentarily lost in a familiar fathomless black hole of hopelessness and grief, The sense of loss of a priceless way of life she would never know. Inconsolable, sorrow tore through her. She envisioned a tidal wave reaching shore and erasing, leaving only nothingness in its wake. She trembled, wiped a single hot tear.

"Indians on the Coast, like elsewhere, weren't treated well, rarely given jobs. It must have been hard. If you could pass for white, you did it. Then you could get work, and your family could eat. You could choose to fight in a war without being made to revoke your Indian status.

"I understand now why my father didn't embrace his heritage. But it made it damned hard for me to make that journey to my Nativeness. It also made it impossible for me not to! Like water, I had to seek and carve. And like a deep current, push and pull my identity out of an unknown depth."

The server interrupted.

"One Seafood Tower for two. Chilled smoked salmon. Fresh oysters. Chilled prawns. Seafood bowl with clams, mussels, prawns, salmon and halibut in lemongrass coconut broth. And alder-grilled bannock bread. Alder-grilled sockeye, halibut and prawns, with tomato and eggplant confit and grilled asparagus."

He put it down with a flourish.

"I could never stop searching. For my Native self. I immersed myself in my cultures. Went deep, into the languages, the beliefs. I found our village on the Coast. What our language was called. I went and shared it with my father. Tears ran down his face. It was the only time I ever saw him cry. He was silent a long time. I stood there with my heart in my mouth. Then finally, he said, "I should have known you would be the one to find this out. You are the one with the dreams. We are from the Coast north of Vancouver."

She finally looked to the food and took an oyster. He watched her take another couple. She shook her head, looking down.

"So many people I've met ask me to help them satisfy the same yearning. How on earth do they sense that I can help them get home? Some who ask are Sixties Scoop kids, adopted out. Some, like me, had parents who thought they could forget being Native. But somewhere, their Indianness, even a generation or two later, shape-shifts and spills out, floods, until the person's heart and spirit drives them forward to know. Who they are, where they're from. An elder once said to me, 'It isn't about blood quantum. It's about having the receivers built in to get those transmissions – those messages from your people in the next world.' I loved that."

Ray was nodding and let go of her hand to serve himself some salmon.

"So, I became a 'home finder' for people who remind me of the waves of a strong, changing tide. Pushed forward and pulled back until they beach on the shore of their truth. This is why I love the Charlie family. They welcomed me. Never questioned my identity. I loved how everyone up North knows exactly how they're related. Right out to about sixth cousins! Let's enjoy the rest of this food now."

He smiled, his mouth evidently full. Leah wanted to climb over the table, wriggle into his lap, and kiss him stupid. She wanted to take him home again. She knew she could drive her fear away when she was on top of him.

"Leah, I'm flying out at five tomorrow. Can we finish the interview? I'd like to spend a bit of time on the North. How the Tlingit-Tagish cultures impacted a woman from the Saltwater People."

"I'm surprised you know that name. Yes, we can certainly do that. I have time tomorrow. If you like, I can give you a lift to the airport."

Leah felt ridiculously happy. She hadn't felt like this for a long time, hopeful, and she wanted much, much more.

Chapter Eleven

Today
Saturday? (I am losing track). I am thinking about identity. I won-
der about how things were back in the days before colonization, how
every culture was distinct. Our cultures have become homogenized, in
some ways. I think homogenization is good for milk. Most of us are
lactose intolerant. Like so many Coastal Indians I know have a
dreamcatcher in their car, even though they were created by Plains
people. Out of the belief that their nightmares could be caught. Not
disturb their spirits in their sleep. Yet even lots of white folks have
them. Are they trying to prevent having awake nightmares while
driving?

All of us are homogenized, especially urban Indians. I don't know if
this is bad or good – it just makes me feel it wasn't so much that way in
the past. People had their unique languages, regalia. You could tell who
someone was by what they wore.

Salish were Salish and practised Big House and their unique sacred
ways. They had their own purification ceremony.

I guess long ago, if we visited the territory of the Plains people, they
may have invited us into a sweat lodge, and to a Sundance or other
sacred ceremonies. By the sounds of it, all the Nations had their own
practises, some were similar. Dakota Sioux Sundance. There, I met lots
of different people from all kinds of Nations. I asked a Nish woman if
their dance was practised the same way. She told me the differences, and
they were many. The Cree people again have a similar ceremony; but
again, the way is different.

At least with the homogenized Nations, one thing I know that remains unchanged. We are not selfish with our ceremonies. Long ago, visitors and those who were adopted from elsewhere could attend. This is the same now. There is controversy, though.

☙

Leah was a little relieved that this would be the last day with Ray. She was falling for him and hard. She knew it was too soon after Phil. She didn't want to think about that. She needed a little time. Time to sit with that journal. To watch those reels that were calling to her. The few she had seen had catapulted her back in time. Created a longing to know what it was she was not able to recall. The strange and unknown reason that she could not remember writing in the old journal. She heard Ray in the shower, singing.

Needing to write out some thoughts, she pulled her new journal to her.

☙

I'm feeling lost, but don't want to think about that. I long for ceremony. Some believe whites should not be allowed to practise any ceremonies, let alone lead them. Some believe they should not be allowed to attend. If I had my own ceremonies, I would just listen to the Old Ones and do as they guided me.

In ceremony, you must face your fear. I have so much fear these days, would I be able to face it? Courageously? I hope that's what ceremony people are doing nowadays, not just inviting whites because they have more money than Indians. Like that guy running a Sundance who charged people $3,000 to attend or be part of it. That's something

78

disturbing. Some mainstream people don't value anything that does not come with a price.

Our ceremonies come with a huge price that Indians know about. Responsibility. The knowledge that we are carrying the ceremony all year long. They don't just last a certain number of days. We know we must conduct ourselves like we are in ceremony all year long. That's why I have avoided them – holy people. They're just far too much work to be around. It's far too much pressure to behave for that length of time. Maybe truly becoming who we are, really who we are, is ceremony. Maybe that's the most sacred ceremony of them all. Maybe this is the ceremony I need, to become who I truly am. How do I do that when so much of me is missing?

જી

Ray was making her breakfast. Something inside her nagged like a raven voice. "Look, look, look" but, so far, she could not see. It was relentless. She was driven. Driven to know why. Why was a piece of her lost? It was truly eerie. Each time she thought of it, she felt electricity fly up from her feet to her brain. The jolt propelled her to find the answers. For now, she would spend the last day with Ray, take him to the airport. This evening, she would get back to the films, to the journal. She would miss him. Badly.

She was absolutely determined to retrieve herself. The answer lay within. The journal and films would help her to reclaim the truth. The young Cree man's face drifted before her. She recalled his words. But was hers a truth she wanted to know? It almost didn't matter. She had to. She had to know.

જી

Ray had breakfast all laid out when she walked, wet-haired, into the kitchen. "I could get used to this." He looked away and did not answer. Her heart sank a little.

She was checking her texts when she said, "Okay, hike and coffee? Or a final interview in a new coffee house?"

"Hike and coffee, definitely!"

"I'll take you to Lynn Canyon."

"I like the name. I'm in your hands."

Feeling vulnerable, Leah was in deep now; could not draw herself back. She now knew why moths were drawn to flames. Not helpless, not unable – only unwilling to resist a lure. She had knowingly dived into this fire, without fear, compelled. There was no way back from her strong feelings for Ray now. She felt him looking at her as she drove across the Lions Gate Bridge. He looked away and down, trying to imagine what this land looked like before contact, just a few hundred years ago.

"Tell me about yourself, Ray; I've been doing an awful lot of talking."

"Well, okay, what is it you'd like to know?"

"About growing up, your family, how you experienced being a mixed blood. Or," she laughed, "as I like to call it, an exotic hybrid."

"I was a bit of a weird kid."

"How so?"

"I loved the bush, wandered all around for miles on my own."

"Sounds idyllic."

"Not in bear country." They both laughed at the Native-style joke, alluding to a thing, allowing her to come to her own conclusion. "I seem to attract them, but I don't really like to."

She grinned at his wording. He fell serious again, trying to articulate.

"I love my mother and sisters; I love the women in my family, in my clan. I love the strength, the humour, the bossiness, the knowing they have about what's right and what's wrong. I love it when they tell me what to do. Wolf women just have that way of knowing, and I am glad I got that, and that I can appreciate how they guide me."

Leah smiled encouragingly at him, focused on the off-ramp.

"My father is quiet. My brother is a lot like him. Both Mom and Dad wanted more children, but my mother couldn't after my little brother; it just about killed her.

"I didn't see Mom's family much. Dad insisted we live in his home village. I don't know really why Mom agreed. You know how unusual is in the North for the woman to follow the man. My parents were not as traditional as others, although they did continue all the practises of the land. Like fish camp and such. My sisters are a blast. We always had a lot of fun. They were older, so my brother and I were their dolls."

Leah knew what this meant. Indian jokes were about letting you see in your imagination. Ray shook his head ruefully.

"My sisters still tease my brother and me within an inch of our lives. But you know how it is with Indians. How they show they love us."

"My sisters got educations, but they came back home to work in the village. They're pretty attached to the place. My brother and I live in Whitehorse. We're very close, live in the same apartment building, see each other every day. In fact, we don't lock our doors. It's easier because we're always back and forth.

"We both go home to the village a lot. Mom isn't well anymore, she had a stroke, hasn't been the same since."

"I'm sorry, that's hard."

"It really is. She can't do what she used to. It's pretty tough on her. My sisters are pretty wonderful. They involve her in everything. They pretend they don't know much, ask her a lot of questions. Like if they're cleaning fish, they'll go through it with her step-by-step. She plays along. It's sweet.

"Dad still hunts. They still go out to fish camp. Though my sisters take direction from Mom, she doesn't say much. We can tell she has a hard time sitting and watching when there are things to be done."

Leah took the off-ramp to West Vancouver. Not liking how far the housing had crawled up the mountain to the edge of the parklands.

Ray didn't notice the change of direction. He was back in the wall tent at the fish camp, remembering.

"You know, I used to envy people who moved around, travelled from place to place. I wanted to see all those places I read about. But there, out at fish camp, or at the hunting cabin, there's this deep feeling of being connected and part of something that is enduring. That makes me glad I grew up the way I did. It wasn't perfect, we didn't always have what we wanted. But Mom and Dad always made sure we never went hungry and tried to make sure we had all we needed.

"I grew up like most kids in villages, listening to CBC North. Batteries for the radio were a number one on the shopping list!"

Leah remembered the importance of the news, and that one and only lifeline to the world – "outside," as Yukoners always referred to anyplace outside the Yukon.

"So, I always wondered how they did that radio thing. How voices came out of the little black box, when all you did was put batteries in it? In grade four, we had a choice of where to go on a field trip to Whitehorse. Of course, there weren't many places to go. We'd already seen the museum, Miles Canyon, the fish ladder. I suggested a tour of the CBC. I was so excited! I couldn't wait. We got off the bus in our town clothes – I had one set of clothes that was only for town. I remember pulling up on the Fourth Avenue and seeing the CBC Radio sign. I don't know what I expected."

He shook his head.

"It seemed so small, but I was absolutely captivated. The walls of equipment, the huge microphones hanging like big spiders from the ceiling. It amazed me that a man was sitting in one of those studios, speaking into the microphone, and it was being heard in cabins and on traplines, and in wall tents all over the territory. That magic I fell in love with right there. I knew what I wanted to do. I had to come outside to study broadcasting. I loved every part of it.

"After training at CHON-FM, the Native station in Whitehorse – oh, of course you know it – I had my mind set to work at the Haines Junction community radio station, since no full-time job was open in Whitehorse. It was such a blast – if someone didn't like what I was playing, they'd stomp right in and tell me, 'Take that thing off right now!' I learned not to mute the microphone; the listeners got a kick out of that live comedy, because they could recognize the voice. There was one drunk guy that hated anything but old country music. I didn't like old country; I'd heard enough of it growing up! This guy would come unhinged every time I played anything else. We got to be good friends. He taught me to have an appreciation for old country. I volunteered at first, and finally got a job at CHON. But CBC felt like the big fish.

"It took a long time, but I made friends there. And by the time there was a retirement, I pretty much told them I was taking over the job, and I did. I love it. Nothing about it is boring. I get to pretty much do what I want with my show. This piece we are working on? Whitehorse is working on getting it aired nationally."

Leah's heart skipped and sped. She was not sure she was ready for that but said nothing. She merged the vehicle onto the Upper Levels Highway. Cypress Provincial Park. She needed the mountains today.

"I changed my mind," she said, "about the canyon. There are too many people there, and it isn't as if the two of us haven't seen our share of rivers. This'll be a good hike; the view is lovely at the top. We could both use some mountain air today."

Ray smiled, gave her the universal Indian nod, chin up.

They climbed in silence. A good silence. Inhaled sweet alpine air. It was a perfect day for a hike, cool with no rain. No other hikers on the way up. They took it slow; he could tell by her breathing that she had asthma. It was wonderful to be up high and still climbing. The sun came out. She looked around at the low alpine fauna. Up here the sun was warm, almost hot. The air was clean, holding the fragrance of a hundred layers of green.

"You know, this really reminds me of home." She stopped. With her arm she made an arc, motioning to the path ahead and the bushes on the right.

"It's almost a Yukonesque view at the top as long as you aren't looking ocean side."

When they were near the top, they turned from the ocean vista across the strait, and breathed in the sweet air of the mountains facing north. Even here you could catch the scent of the sea. Coastal mountains for as far as the eye could see. It was here and then that Leah gathered her courage, reached out, took Ray's hand as they stood in silence. He did not resist but curled his hand around hers as they stood together lost in their own thoughts; drinking in the magnificence falling at their feet before them. Her heart rose and flew far away toward the sea.

☙

MOON OF THE WITCH, *Verse Three*

Blue with fear I double back again
I'm running blind
With that old dog at my heels
I've never run that way.
Still deaf to the only voice
My mind is wrong, oh
But my heart must be right
And it's here I start to pay…

☙

Leah was hot, flushed from an erotic dream. She showered and was still left aroused. She dressed warmly, picked up the journal and her pen and went outside to write.

☙

Today
In the garden, I'm watching two squirrels manically tearing across the ground, up a tree, leaping to another tree, then tearing down the trunk. They speak to one another in frantic chatters and whirrs. Why are they rushing? A crow hovers. Flies close above one squirrel, who has become frozen on the ground. The crow hovers still lower, just barely above the

85

squirrel. The squirrel stands upright and takes a swipe at the crow. The crow simply moves higher, hovers just out of reach, as if he is saying, "Look what I can do that you can't." I laugh out loud and watch as they continue this little dance. The crow seems to take delight in distracting the squirrel from his quest to tear about. I guess Crow has nothing better to do. He sits now above the squirrel uttering strange dolphin-like chattering, as the squirrel warns with a staccato rattle that sounds aggressive.

Now the crow meows, over and over. I wonder if they learned that from cats, or if that is a natural sound. Maybe he is taunting the squirrel, who surely is afraid of cats. In any case, I can't stop laughing.

It makes the pain go away for a few minutes, but soon it returns to cloak around my shoulders. I think it would take dynamite to move the pain off me for good.

☙

She woke from a dream she could not pull out of. She lay in the grey morning light trying to understand the meaning. She recalled sitting in the cabin. Uncle Angus had come in the door, with a wide smile. She had run into his arms, crying out, "Uncle, oh Uncle, I thought you were dead."

"No, I am not dead, my girl. Understand? Just someplace else."

In the dream she did know. She felt the oneness of the two worlds, with no separation.

"Uncle, can you help me?"

"I will always help you."

"I need to remember, Uncle. I have lost some of my memory."

"Are you ready?"

"I think I am."

"You sure?"

"No, I'm afraid."

"Fear chases it away. Face the fear. Make friends, ask it what it wants."

"Okay, Uncle. I miss you, Uncle. So much my heart feels like it's been torn in two. It hurts."

"I know."

"How can I stop hurting?"

"You can't. It's life, like weather. Dress for the weather."

They sat in silence, and he embraced her, saying it was time for him to go take care of Gramma. When he held her she smelled his jacket, as she always had. And as always, it smelled of the outside. The lake, the spruce trees, the thousands of medicines of the land she loved.

This was what was troubling her. What had he meant, "Dress for the weather?" And how was she going to face her fear when all she wanted to do was run as far away from it as she could?

ॐ

Today

The water on the inlet moves west to east like it has a plan. The insistent bird was calling, "See? See? See?" As soon as I heard the message, it stopped. Ravens were here somewhere earlier. They only said, "Why? Why?" That's what I'd like to know – why! When I heard, they left. Their voices sounded like those of old and treasured friends. When I opened the window and asked them to speak again, they would not.

The sun is trying to shine through marble clouds. Flash-frozen lightning. Naked trees against that sky, black delicate filigree. A solitary duck follows the water west to east now, silently flies, wings drumming a fast beat. Damp leaves, heavy with wet, cannot move on a restless wind.

One mad squirrel machine-gun repeating, "This, this, this, this, this, this!" A tiny chickadee throws in a few words. "Look!"

The other squirrel on the ground is focused on his frantic-looking foraging work. They remind me of me, foraging for my truth.

❧

Still lost in the meaning of the dream, cheeks flushed, Leah needed no blush this morning. She dropped the tin of Lavazza coffee all over the floor. Already late, she left it and ran for the shower. She was out of shampoo. Soap would have to do. Her frustration mounted, knowing how hard her hair was going to be to comb out. How had she fallen for a man who clearly had no real feelings for her? How could she have allowed herself to be that vulnerable to believe that he did?

Stepping out of the shower, she found no towel. Remembering it was in the bedroom, she ran and slipped on the tile, slamming down, bruised her hip. Cursing by the time she was rushing into her clothes, she tore the only pair of stockings she had.

"For the love of God, can anything else go wrong?"

A briefing with the Federal Minister and his Provincial counterpart was not something she could be late for, she would hail taxi. She dialled and was on hold for minutes. Tears of frustration burned her eyes. She put the phone on speaker, dropped it on the bed and found a pantsuit. Dated, but it didn't require stockings. The cab was late. She tossed a $20-dollar bill over the seat into the driver's lap before grasping her briefcase and tearing into the building. At least when she flashed her door pass, security didn't stop her. The elevator had an "Out of Order" sign. She groaned.

Taking the stairs as quickly as she could, she was sweaty and gasping by the time she reached the fifth floor. She struggled in the door and ran straight into Jean, her coffee buddy.

"God, Jean, I'm late for a briefing. Do I look alright?"

"You're gorgeous. Just dab the perspiration before you go in."

She found a tissue in her purse, wiped at her face, took a breath. She could see through the frosted glass that they were already in the Deputy's office. She took a deep breath, knocked and walked in as coolly as she could.

"I'm so sorry I was delayed. I had one of those mornings."

Her Deputy Minister was frowning, gave her a tight smile seemingly for appearances. The Provincial Minister was deadpan. She shook his hand and introduced herself. It was then she realized she had left her briefing binder at home. Panic moved like a gale force wind through her. She could do this. Somehow, she would have to pull it off. She booted her notebook, retrieving the agenda from her email.

"Miss Red Sky, we were just discussing the Indigenous Youth Execution."

Leah felt as though she'd been struck. She looked at the first item on the agenda. Youth execution? It seemed so absurd, awful. Her nerves got to her. She began to laugh uproariously. The Ministers stared at her, cold. Worse, there was no way she could get control herself. Her laughter was a runaway train, fuelled by their indifference.

It was minutes before she could compose herself. But in that time, something snapped. Frustration and fury, fuelled by weeks of fear, rose like a tidal wave, sucking the wisdom like water right off the beach. The wave crashed in with a vengeance.

"So, how are these Youth Executions going to be carried out?" Leah spat. "I don't recommend smallpox blankets this time around, because, no doubt, someone will catch on. I mean seriously, who the hell would put 'Indigenous Youth Execution' on an agenda? How ignorant can people in Indigenous Relations be?"

"It was actually me." Her Minister had ice chips for eyes.

"I see. Well. I know we are talking about a youth strategy and how to roll it out, but seriously? Could you have picked worse wording? As an Indigenous woman and staff member, I find this highly insensitive, inappropriate, and downright insulting. I would like an apology."

The Provincial Minister was looking at his nails.

"Miss Red Sky, I certainly will NOT apologize."

"Is it because I have bigger balls than you? The fact that I wear them on my chest is no reason to be arrogant about this."

"Miss Red Sky, take your things and go home. I think your time with the Ministry is just about over."

Leah stood and stared at her.

"With pleasure, you fat, arrogant, inept cow."

The Provincial Minister's lips were twitching. She saw a glint of laughter in his eyes. With as much dignity as she could, she nodded to him, glared at her Minister, and left. She was face to face with Jean's horrified expression. It was only then that she realized she had been shouting.

꧂

"Ray?"

"Leah, hi!" She ignored the pleasure in his voice. She ignored it. Clearly, he wasn't who she had thought he was. He'd been in it for the sex. He hadn't called her since leaving Vancouver.

"I wanted to know if we have any loose ends to tie up with the project. If so you, can call anytime from now on – I lost my position with the Ministry."

"Yes, so I gathered from your email. Is that a good thing?"

"Well, not from the standpoint of my finances, but yes, it is from the standpoint of my ethics."

"Your email description was hilarious; sorry there were consequences. I have to say, I wish I'd been a fly on the wall," he chuckled quietly. "Leah, you are some character – if I come back down to Vancouver, I just have to get to know you better. I need some kinda whatever it is that you got! I am just way too tame!" (*Yeah, I know what it is you want that I've got.*)

"Well, maybe tame isn't a bad thing." (*Keep it light.*)

"Personally, I like my women like my coffee. Strong and bitter."

Leah's laugh sounded bitter even to her. Ray did not miss her tone, but at least she no longer seemed so angry at him. It wasn't a good thing to have a Wolf woman angry at you.

CHAPTER TWELVE

Leah has one perfectly preserved and beautiful memory that comforts her spirit. She keeps reliving it.

Uncle and Haywire are outside, she hears them talking.

"Come on, Chaos, the ice will melt!" Leah's excited, like a little kid, can't wait to get moving. She smiles to herself and calls, "I'm coming, just grabbing mitts!"

Doris has a filthy look on her face, is shaking her head. Leah isn't measuring up. She feels Doris's judgement coming at her like a bad smell. She hears every day, "A good woman can run fishnets in winter with bare hands. You think you can do that, city girl?" Leah feels frustration rise. She sees the dark look in Doris's eyes, and knows Doris does not approve of Leah being with her son. Doris is trying, but Leah knows it's only to keep peace with Haywire. Leah can feel the resentment coming off Doris in waves when he's not looking.

She smiles and says "Bye!" to a grumpy Doris, pulls her mitts on, and throws her scarf around her neck, tying it tight.

They're waiting outside the back door. She breathes in air redolent of spruce, moss, frozen berries. Doris is glaring at her through the kitchen window, but she will not show that she feels it. Leah can't help herself, turns and sticks her tongue out. Then just as Doris's face scowls, it changes into a broad smile and Leah sees the wave. She knows Haywire has changed that look. He pretends he does not see this tension between the two women, but he teases Leah out of earshot.

"What did you do to Mom? Pee in the mush? Chip her stove? Insult Hank Williams?"

They take the well-worn path behind the house, heading for the meadows, and she can't wait to see this place Haywire has talked so much about. Her feet crunch on frozen moss, layers of fallen pine needles. The ground has no give. As if the permafrost has reached with icy fingers all the way to the surface. The air is stinging cold on her ears, her face. Her breath clouds with every exhale.

Angus walks ahead, with his .30-30. This is not a hunting trip, but guns are part of life because, as Angus says, "Never know."

Leah is walking in the middle behind Uncle. Haywire behind her, carries a.22. They don't make a sound when they walk but, no matter how hard Leah tries, she makes noise as they weave through the spruce, jack pines and buck brush. Leah tries hard, but her feet keep breaking sticks. Haywire hisses, "Why don't you scare *all* the game away?" She turns and shoots him a look. He grins widely as she trips on a deadfall.

She finds looking at Angus's back comforting. He always wears the same plaid wool cap, army-green bush jacket, loose khaki pants. Bush boots, leather lace-ups, high on the ankle, pants tucked in.

They move around willows, through thickets of buck brush, and finally now the land is clear and flat for miles around, except for stands of trees with a few deep gold leaves here and there. The day is crisp with dry cold, and though there isn't a sign of snow down low, the feel is in the air, as if the mountains breathe through their snow cover, and exhale across the valley.

She hears a stream before she sees it.

"Okay," Uncle says quietly, and puts his packsack down. The little lake is ahead of them, a pond, really. Solid ice. Uncle pulls a coffee tin out of his sack. It has a wire handle. Fills the can in the nearby stream. He takes a drink, and the water drips down the side of the can to his canvas jacket. He motions to them, and Leah takes a drink because it is offered, not because she is thirsty.

The water is clear, cold, sweet. She smiles at Uncle, who smiles back his gentle smile. Haywire collects wood and is piling small sticks. She hears the fire's first words and turns to see Haywire building it up. She moves to it, spreads her hands, enjoying the heat.

Uncle kneels with Haywire, puts the tin right on the flames. She notices how he and Haywire have no need to talk while they work together.

In a few minutes the water is boiling, and Uncle takes a handful of coffee grounds out of a paper bag from his packsack, throws them in the bubbles. Leah watches as the grounds disappear into the water and catches their fragrance. Uncle fetches a cup of water out of the stream in a tin cup. Leah watches as he adds it to the tin.

"Uncle, what is that for?"

"Sink the grounds so you don't gotta chew them." He grins. The brew comes back to a boil and Uncle hooks the wire with the stick he has been turning in his hands. He takes two tin cups out of his pack and fills them. "Here, go ahead." He passes her a steaming enamel mug. She sips it; the rich fragrance in the steam.

"This is the best coffee I ever had, Uncle. What kind is it?"

"Campfire coffee."

"I mean the brand, Uncle."

"Dunno, the cheap one," he laughs.

Leah savours the contrast of the scalding hot drink in the cold air. She knows no matter how much money she pays and how fancy the beverage is named, this is the perfect coffee. She savours each sip until it is gone. It warms her belly. The warmth spreads through her chilled body.

"May I have more, Uncle?"

"Why, shore," he says. He pours from the tin into her cup. He always says, "Why, shore" and laughs. She wonders if it is a line from an old cowboy movie. He only has about three expressions. This is one. The other is, "Wanna fight?" Always said with his two fists up in a boxing stance. He often randomly asks her this. She knows it's to make her laugh, and she always does. It's cute. The other expression comes with a thoughtful look, "Maybe, too."

Now Leah watches Haywire lace on a pair of black skates. His bladed feet make awkward steps over the snow toward the ice; she imagines a baby moose struggling to walk. He skates around, and Angus and she watch. After a while he comes over and says, "Uncle, have a go." Uncle Angus grins. He puts his cup down near the fire, laces the skates and makes his way to the pond. He skates, pushing one leg out behind the other, faster, faster, still. She watches his breath leave a steamed cloud behind him. He comes back, removes the skates, hands them to Leah.

"Your turn," says Haywire. Leah does not hesitate. She pulls off her boots, feeling the cold nipping her toes, and laces the skates up tight. She hasn't skated outside in years. Walking to the pond, she is careful not to trip, stepping tentatively onto the ice. She stands, looking down. It's like glass: She can see all the way to the bottom, the little creatures walking about, little fish swimming, and the weeds standing, undisturbed. It's breathtaking. She moves as if she is skating on air, suspended, on this perfect ice, pure magic. She has never been able to skate this fast on girls' skates or keep her ankles from bending. She spins around, finds this like flying, like drifting, like she is a leaf on the surface of the creek. It's a moment she wants to last forever. Suspended between the sky and water, on this thin frozen crust of ice. Breathless, she stops and kneels on the ice to see the life below. She is elated, peaceful, happy.

❧

September 24, 1993
Johnnie got a job surveying up on the Dempster Highway being built from Dawson City to Tuktoyaktuk. He writes his girlfriend letters on rolls of orange survey tape with black markers. They're tough to read, but we all enjoy them.

Sammy doesn't care about working, and never has much money. But he'll gladly give you his last five bucks, if he thinks you need it more than he does. Haywire got work hauling gravel down at Johnsons Crossing.

Now that I'm back in Whitehorse, Sammy watches over me now that Haywire is gone. I love all these guys, but they drive me nuts sometimes. Last week, when Johnnie was down from the Dempster, I was trying to sleep, and they were drinking. He and Sammy insisted on coming in my room and giving me chips to eat because I wasn't out partying with them in the living room. Hahahaha – they dumped them right on the sheets. I'm still brushing the crumbs out!

❧

Leah met Ray for a few hours on his follow-up visit to Vancouver. She had cooled herself enough to shut down any feelings of attraction, having replaced it with a cold deep anger.

"Look, Ray, would you turn off the recorder?" He looked disappointed but did.

96

He wanted her. He didn't know how to make a move after obviously pissing her off with that statement about her body. She seemed so much more distant. There was a voice emerging. With it, a feisty yet sage expression in her eyes. That kept him from trying to initiate anything.

She spoke with her entire being as if it were a ceremony, as he had seen the elders do. "It's hard to be a white Indian. To be asked by Indians what my Nation is and be told by white people that I don't look Indian. I usually say, 'What kind of Indian don't I look like?' Then if you're misguided enough, like I was, to work for government, you're expected to speak on behalf of every Indian in Canada.

"I worked at the Aboriginal Friendship Centre here in Vancouver. There were the random calls. White people used to phone up and say things like 'Wow, you sound really educated.' To which I would reply, 'Well, yeah. Some of us are.' They didn't know how insulting that was. They'd try to backtrack pretty hard.

"Others would move you by asking, 'I found an eagle feather, what does that mean?' Because they were so sincere, I tried to be kind to them, because it took a lot of courage for them to make the call."

"Our relationship with non-Natives has never been easy, has it?"

"It puts us mixed-bloods in an interesting quandary. We're the evidence of the troubled relationship. But there are the moniyâw, skiŋčáačəɬ, kutchen, who come with respect. They say, 'I know you can help me with a problem I have and, if you can't, I know you know someone who can.' Some of our own people don't have that reverence for Knowledge Keepers.

"I remember one of my exes. Oh, my God! I thought if I was with another Saulteaux, I'd learn about my culture. Ha. He'd come unhinged if I mentioned the word 'Indian' or 'culture.' If I really wanted him to lose it, all I had to say was the word 'prayer.' It was extraordinary. How deep his internalized racism was. I called him a Redneck Redman and threatened to make him a T-shirt."

"That's hilarious and tragic." Ray was trying to figure out how to get Leah back to her place.

"I really should have. He reminded me of my father. My father did me a favour, though, when the dead Indians started showing up, playing tricks, scaring the bejeezus outta me. My dad was a really against Indians kind of guy. I mean, to the point where he hid being Indian from us, like we were not going to find out. Well, the cosmic joke was on him. In my adolescence, I started to have these profound encounters. I had to tell somebody, so I told him."

"Up North, the Old are always watching and listening to the little kids, for those gifts,' Ray said. "To see whose spirit has come back in them."

"Yeah, when I told my dad, he was forced to fess up that we were Native. It was either that or get me a psychiatrist – and he was far too afraid of that idea, apparently."

"You have such a funny way of expressing yourself."

"I don't mean to; this stuff is serious. My father gave me one piece of good advice. He said to never be afraid of my gifts, and never let my fear control me. He insisted I had to learn to control my gifts, never let them control me."

"Some of my family have had some wild encounters. Gotta be strong to handle those."

"I've had some good teachers over the years. Like at Sundance. But that teaching from Dad was the one that set my feet on the path, got me to deal with those experiences. That advice is seriously the only good thing I got from him – besides my bad attitude. Dad was a great teacher – he taught me what *not* to do by doing it. Those kinds of teachings are truly the most powerful. But you have to get past the pain, the trauma to see those gifts. His advice changed my life. I would have gone on thinking I was nuts. Instead, I began working with my gifts. It was hard to know or feel or see things that people were trying desperately to hide. People sensed I could see. They often hate me, and fear me, no matter how kind I tried to be. Like my ex, Phil," she said softly.

Ray nodded. "I know. My sister has been through that, with people that aren't very, uh, let's say…healthy."

"Yeah, those dead Indians who visit me, they have a sense of humour. Play tricks, say the funniest things in my dreams. I've been told I laugh a lot in my sleep. I often wake myself up laughing. But these days, I kinda wish they would all go on some kind of vacation, a spirit cruise."

Ray was grinning widely. "You should write a screenplay."

"I need a break from them. They follow me. I mean, everywhere."

ℭ

September 29, 1993
We walked all the way to the junction yesterday and stopped in where Uncle Angus lives with Gramma. I sat in her room and held her hand for two hours, and we didn't say anything. There was no need. She is tiny!

Haywire and Uncle drank a couple of pots of tea. I loved sitting with Gramma Maisey! She is the gentlest woman. She has a new house that Indian Affairs built. It's pretty nice. Nobody has much furniture, just a kitchen table and a couple of chairs, and beds. Her stove is a real beauty. It's big enough to heat the house and cook on. I wish we lived this close to water! They have a stream running by, just at the bottom of the little slope the house is on. The house is surrounded by pine trees, and it's lovely and quiet here. Not right on the road like Doris's place.

We also met Uncle Timmy. His place is really old. He was married to Joyce. He's from Old Crow, so he talks differently. I love his accent!

He dresses like its 1950. He's got the old high-waisted, pleated baggy pants, a huge bill on his cap, and the kind of plaid shirt that men wore, buttoned all the way up. I love to listen to how he talks.

The third place we visited was Auntie Laylie's. She is Doris and Angus's sister. Wow. I wish she was Haywire's mom! She's sweet, kind, and has soft gentle eyes and a sad smile. She has a LOT of kids!! It was lovely to meet them all and be around kids again. They have a log cabin with two rooms, a kitchen and one huge bedroom. But again, how do they all share one bedroom?

Same thing, just a table and chairs and beds. They have a stove like Gramma's in the kitchen, a real beauty that can cook and heat, too. They dry meat on a string above the stove. There are a bunch of strings where there were a dozen drying mitts and boot liners.

CHAPTER THIRTEEN

Leah seemed unaware of the path she was on, but Ray felt he knew the direction. He was longing for the voice to emerge that he found so erotic. The one he loved to hear. He was patient, but he was running out of days.

Leah was free-talking. Aware that Ray wanted her. Not caring. She didn't want him, not anymore. Not without a future. Now, she only needed to feel heard.

Ray interjected at times. Later her words haunted him. He regretted being sexual with her.

"My family created a portal that brought the spirits of agony and sorrow into the house each night. There was an awful dance of destruction until dawn."

Ray nodded. He could feel the truth of this in Leah's cadence, punctuated with what sounded very much like unwritten song lyrics.

"Listening to you is like listening to a traditional language. Poetic."

"I feel like my Mom, like water. Mom just is. She has flowing, quiet strength. Easy to see as a doormat. If you think strength has to be aggressive. Mom is more like a willow.

"Mom forgave every terrible word and act, right as it was happening.

"Dad was not who he wanted to be. In truth, he was a gifted poetic soul. And then there were times when he was so sweet-spirited. He would tell me a story of his father with so much love and longing that I swore I could see the world through my grand-father's eyes, feel how it was for my father to be in his presence. He could make my soul dance – and then raze it to the ground. Mom allowed his storms to move her like driftwood, letting the storm render her into art as it carried her.

"Mom has always been a willow – they grow only in or near water. They're humble. Fragile, compared to other trees. But willows bend, and bend, and bend some more, and not break. I learned from Mom to bend like a willow.

"From Dad I learned to be like water. I flow from all my ancestral directions into myself. I learned this because he couldn't do it. In fact, resisted, with all his storm-filled being.

"I can imagine the water of my different ancestral selves. Seeking across dry ground from east, west, north, and south. Carrying the powdered earth from the directions with it. The water is the tears of joy, of sorrow, of the Old Ones. The silt is the genes. The tears and cells come, flow together, unite into one within me."

"Another song!" Ray said. It was as if she didn't hear him.

"I'm not sure reconciliation with non-Indigenous people is possible, because colonization isn't over. We're still 'Indians' under the Indian Act. The only people in the country who have 'registration' cards. What about those who don't fit the guide-lines? Their label is 'non-status.' Called something because of what they're not! And I will be non-status until I make a decision about registering Non-Indian one minute, Indian the next. I'm so conflicted.

"It's bizarre, how others define us. I have enough trouble with defining my own identity. I could get a status card, but I don't. Why get 'benefits' for being Native. Benefits. What an oxymoron!"

Ray had never really thought about it. His Nation had settled land claims. The North was a different world: If you were "part" Native, you were Native. If you were connected by blood to a Nation, that *was* your identity. He stared at his hands around the paper cup, and at the table below; caught himself staring through it. He was listening that intently. He noticed a Native carving underneath the glass. He looked up again, smiled at Leah as she silently looked off at nothing in the distance. She looked tired.

He still wanted her, badly. His groin ached. He didn't want to ask only to hear "No."

ᐤᐤ

Coyote catches the scent of smoke, dog, humans. Instinct conflicts with a new hunger. Curious, fearless, he skulks closer. The odour of human tickles his nostrils, makes him turn away, sneeze. The smell of dog is unbearably alluring. He has encountered these scents before out in the flats, out around the lake. He isn't hungry but has learned to kill for the killing. To prevent that terrible eating-away feeling in his belly, he has learned to take life well before he is hungry.

He creeps in closer, closer. Soundless.

Unaware of danger, the dog does not hear him, sleeps. One leap to the neck. Resignation in its eyes, the dog gives himself. He knows it's time, does not resist. Coyote tastes succulent blood as he wills the life out of the animal. He shakes it, as though it were already lifeless.

Coyote drags the much larger animal into the cover of the bush. The dog's heart takes one last leap, ceases to beat.

He feeds until his belly is too full to eat anymore, then leaves it to trot away to find a safe spot to nap.

CHAPTER FOURTEEN

October 30, 1993

The snow has come. It was like waiting for my moon time to begin. The sky felt heavy for days, the land was ready, waiting. Huge flakes began to fall at dusk and, over the course of about four days, the earth has been hidden by a thick layer of white.

I felt like a child, waking to a silent, snow-covered world. It was the silence I heard first, before getting up to look out the window.

One perfect layer, "all the same deep" as Haywire says, everywhere. No drifts, as it fell in uncannily still air. No bitter wind. I walked out in it and stood. Catching ice flakes on my tongue. Formed a perfect snowball. Threw it at the kitchen window. Well, it was supposed to hit below it, but my aim isn't all that good. Doris did not look pleased. Of course, I giggled furiously and had to gain control before going back in.

This early morning, the sky brassy blue, the world filled with sun sparkles. Suddenly everything felt lighter. I went out back and saw each branch of each tree and bush covered in a thick crystal layer of fluff. Winter has transformed the land into another world. It is glittering, brilliant. And it is warmer.

One thing that's weird is that the snow has made me insatiably thirsty.

I was frying potatoes for breakfast when Angus came. When I offered coffee, he said, "Why, Shore." It was the only time he smiled. His brow was furrowed. He said Timmy had started drinking. He showed up at Gramma's house. Haywire said to me to get ready, they're all about to fall like dominoes. I didn't know what he meant.

My sweetheart looked so sad. Then mad, I could tell; his jaw tightened. I didn't ask. Haywire asked Uncle how to set up the traps. Both Angus and Haywire cheered right up as he told us what to do. Step one, go get the traps from the back room down at the lake. Step two, walk and pace out the line, and camo (disguise) the traps, leave bait in them. It's happening!

This afternoon after lunch with Uncle, we took the path that runs across the road from Doris's place down to Little Annie. We walked through the bush for about a half-hour, jumped a creek, and came out down by the lake. The path down is my new favourite place! That, the creek, and coming out at the lake.

We broke trail, and Haywire said it would make walking easier, even if it snows again. Haywire said to be quiet, because there are grizzlies and wolverines all around there. I looked above the forest, and saw their land is surrounded by mountains. They seem to be resting Old Ones who sit, absolutely content to simply be. I want to climb them all, to know them. To see this land from their perspective. To see how they see us.

Haywire wants to set rabbit snares. He pointed out their tiny trails, saying that's where to set them.

He showed me a spot where he said one rabbit danced. I never know when he is serious, so I nodded. I looked at the prints of the back legs, and it did look like it danced. He grinned, shook his head, and whispered, when I offered coffee. "Greenhorn." I just said, "I thought we were supposed to be quiet."

The old family cabin is right beside the lake. This is where Haywire and all the Aunts and Uncles grew up. It was built by Haywire's grandfather. Why, I wonder, didn't Gramma build her new house, here, too? Uncle keeps his traps, his boat and all that down here. The cabin is not large, it's made of logs. I wondered how they all lived in here. In two rooms. We picked up all the small traps and a medium-sized one.

Haywire put half in his pack and half in mine. We're going to scout out a good place for the trapline. It can't be today because I got up too late.

Haywire just wants to try for small game and maybe a lynx. It took me awhile to figure out it was a lynx, because he kept saying "link." He was mad when I corrected him; he hates being corrected. I have to remember not to do that. Mission school ended at the end of grade seven. He chose not to go to F.H. Collins Secondary School in Whitehorse. He's obviously sensitive about it.

Haywire has a bad temper. Really bad. Mostly when I try to tell him about Coyote. He doesn't believe me about how the coyote looks at me, like prey. I tried to say that I was telling him because I feel nervous. But he gets annoyed by me talking about it. When I feel how deep his anger runs, I go very quiet. But I don't understand.

October 9, 1993
It's been awful. First, it was just Timmy drinking. Then Angus came down and said Laylie was asking for us. We went over, and her husband, Ronnie, was drunk. When he was distracted, she asked us to look after the kids. If she doesn't drink with him, he will hurt her. So, we will look in on the kids and make sure they have enough food, water and wood. She says they'll be fine other than that. Now I know why her eyes are sad.

A day later, we heard they were at it. We heard from Uncle that Timmy came down trying to talk him into buying beer.

The next day, Angus didn't show up. Haywire was in a really bad mood. I knew why when we went to visit Gramma. The whole lot of them were partying up there.

Timmy made a move on me, and I ran out crying. I felt horrible. Haywire and I walked into the meadows on the way home and tried to find grouse. Being out there calmed us both down. I imagine this is why he knows the flats so well.

When we got back, Doris was gone. Haywire gritted his teeth and threw his gloves on the floor. He hasn't spoken since. His anger is a beast, skulking around this house.

She came back two days later, and I don't know how she got home. She has stayed drunk.

Last night, she asked me to pull out my guitar and sing her something. I sang her Hank Williams' "Your Cheatin' Heart." Man, I wish I hadn't! ALL night, all we heard was "Your cheatin' heart...", then an hour later, "will make you weep...You'll cry..." And an hour after that, "cry and try to sleep." Oh, my God! It took her all night to drunk-sing that song. Please let this end soon!

October 12,1993
Each day, we check on the kids. They've been getting off to the bus to school okay. We made sure to take fresh meat up for them. They're low on groceries. We'll have to make a run to Whitehorse soon. We hauled water and helped them chop enough wood for a couple of days, and bring it in.

I thought they could use some fun, so asked if they had any sleds to go down the hill on. They hauled out cardboard boxes and garbage bags. We giggled ridiculously sliding down the hill for a couple of hours.

I think they were just really happy for our company. I feel so bad for them. Haywire joined in at the end, and even he started to laugh. Thank God! The anger had me tense, and I was tired of walking on eggshells.

October 15,1993
Well, one by one apparently, they're all sobering up. We went up to check the kids, and found Laylie looking limp and miserable, hanging like a dress on a hanger, drinking days-old tea. (I could tell because it's like there was an oil slick on top.) They had run out of

canned milk. Ronnie was outside grumping around, calling for the kids to get wood and water in.

Haywire had said they would all sober up when the money ran out. I hope so; I want things to be the way they were. No doubt, so do the kids.

October 19, 1993
I had the weirdest thing happen last night I was terrified! First there was a pounding on the door in the middle of the night. Nobody had heard a car or crunching footsteps. Haywire yelled out, "Who's there?!" Nobody answered.

Then I dreamt I was flying – looked down and saw three empty coffins, open, lying in a row.

The next thing I knew I was woken up by someone weightless sitting on my chest, talking to me. I felt it was someone I know. I could see this little grey shape. I froze and couldn't breathe! I woke up Haywire and told him. He didn't say a word, just held me tight. This morning we got up, and damned if both of the bolted doors weren't wide open! Doris just looked at Haywire. A strange look passed between them, but neither said a word. Then Doris went and closed the doors. It's like they think they know something. He's been quiet, and alone in his thoughts.

ॐ

Today
I had this dream between this world and the next: A dragonfly dances in front of me. In that space between, it floats, and there's a shimmer trail behind it of colour. Gold, blue, green, pink. As it dances to and fro, I watch and listen. It's dancing and singing for me.

I need to be very quiet and listen to the song to understand what I need to know. I'm listening as this creature round-dances, side to side. I'm getting the message when I am called back.

Leah recalls the events that followed that entry and cannot stop weeping. She writes in the new journal to stop.

Today
I don't get it. The robins are still here. What made them decide to stick around for the winter? Does it mean winter will be mild, or are the robins confused?

I haven't seen the swans in such a long time. There are four, coming in their usual direction down the lagoon, west to east, which means they've had two young this year.

The mother is graceful. She is in front, followed by a young one, I think, because it's smaller. Behind is another small swan, and the father is at the end. I imagine it's the father, since he is largest.

I love to watch them from a distance, moving as though the current is taking them along. When they are closer, I can see the heads moving slightly forward and backward with the motion of their swimming feet. I love the soft, perfect white of them against the steel grey of the water. It gives me, if only for a few moments, deep peace.

Leah feels deep sadness but cannot stop reading. The old diary thrills and devastates her.

October 20,1993
I can't stop sobbing. We got home after setting up the line in the meadows. Doris was sitting at the table crying, cutting up moose fat. Tears

*pouring down her chubby cheeks. Haywire asked her what was wrong.
It was as if she didn't want to hurt us. She could only say "I heard it on
the radio." Then she quoted CBC.*

*"Samuel Johnny and John Charlie died in a house fire last night,
in a home that burned to the ground in Whitehorse. The fire was
believed to have been started by a cigarette."*

We were just stunned. How could this happen?

Why Sammy and Johnnie? They never hurt a fly.

❦

Leah brewed Labrador tea. The amber colour and fragrance
spoke in whispers of the land she loved, that was so far away.

❦

October 21, 1993

*Today we have to help Uncle haul down meat from the top of a moun-
tain. The moose are taking their time coming down from up high this
year. He says it's because it's still fairly warm.*

*He had skinned and butchered it, and packed a hindquarter out, but
needs all of us to hike up and get the rest down. Haywire says they don't
usually do this, because animals may get at it. He wants to give it to the
Johnny and Charlie families in Whitehorse for the potlatches.*

October 22, 1993

*We went up the mountain yesterday, and they all got ahead of me. My
lungs won't let me climb as fast. It started to snow. Those huge flakes,
that covered the path. So here I was alone, walking through heavy
falling snow and absolute silence, and losing their tracks. I just kept
going. I figured they would find me if I lost their trail. I remembered*

everything Haywire taught me about tracking, and I didn't lose them. I encountered a mean, mangy-looking little coyote. It was breathtaking and terrifying, because I didn't know if he would attack. I thought I was in danger. He must have smelled the meat. I called for Haywire and was relieved when the coyote bolted off. Haywire didn't hear me (the snow sucks up sound), but I finally caught up to the rest of them because they had stopped.

It was hard work to get that meat down off the mountain. I'm filled with wonder at how the Indigenous people here have survived for centuries in this harsh climate.

I was given the ribs, because they know I am not as strong as a Northern woman. They allowed me to pull it down with a rope.

They were laughing and saying to make sure it didn't get ahead of me.

December 30, 1993
All the funerals are done. They were so hard. The people here bury their beloved up high. I don't want to think about all that happened. Sammy had a Catholic funeral and was buried up on Grey Mountain. I'm glad because that's where the wild roses grow in the spring.

Johnnie went to his Mom's village, Champagne. It's tiny, on a corner on the road to Dawson. We had the service in a leaning Anglican church, and walked up a steep hill by the river to bury him. They will put a tent over him. I can't think about that right now.

We finally checked the traps today. They were all sprung, there was blood around them, and coyote tracks. One had a squirrel's foot in it! There's a coyote who has been robbing the traps. We didn't catch him. Haywire says this one is very, very smart. He also says it's like Coyote is playing with us. He wants to catch him so badly.

LETTERS FROM BABYLON, *Verse Two*

One plus one is two, one take away one is nothing
I used to be a poet, but man I ain't no poet now
But I know that tears are sacred
and rage is sacred
and fear is sacred
and losing is sacred
And all this was so beautiful,
it does not seem beautiful now

CHAPTER FIFTEEN

February 1994 (don't know the date; we don't have a year calendar).
Haywire has been gone a month. I miss him so much. I cry myself to sleep
at night. On Haywire's last day off he moved me back to Little Annie.

I was visiting Uncle each day, and helping him at the cabin, and
with whatever he was doing. Now he keeps asking me where the
bruises came from. I can't say it. I can't.

I only remember that Coyote came and caught me when I was alone
at Doris's. I couldn't fight; Coyote is too smart and too strong. I heard
something tear inside my head when he had hold of me, like fabric rip-
ping. I have not told anyone. I have been very sick, and Doris has just
left me to myself.

I can't stop hating. How can I love so much and hate so much?
Mostly I hate myself, because I thought I liked that Coyote, and maybe
that's why he keeps coming!

Two weeks later
Haywire came home. He won't speak to me. He knows. He says I
cheated on him. That's crazy talk! I can't believe he could think that of
me. I can only cry. He's so angry, and Doris heard him, so I'm guessing
she is too. She hasn't said much. Haywire started drinking. I am scared,
so scared! I can feel his seething and I'm waiting for him to blow.

Uncle is the only one who isn't mean. He doesn't say anything, just
loves me how I am.

♀

An undated entry, on the page stains, drops that look like rain, that have run the ink. She knows it is her old tears and feels a deep sense of loss before she sees the words.

She sobs uncontrollably as she reads, fear roaring in her ears. She must know.

☙

Me and Haywire buried the treasure under a tree in the meadow. I am still weak. We left a sign there, so we will always know where it is.

☙

There are no dates from here on in.

What is this ridiculous mention of treasure she has no memory of? All she feels is a terrible sense of dread.

☙

Coyote came again. How can he know when I'm alone? I hate myself for not knowing he was waiting for me. Why did I go use the outhouse? I hate myself for not being able to fight. It took longer this time, a couple of days. I couldn't walk for a long time, and I look worse this time. His bite marks are on me from head to toe. I have other marks, black and purple. I'm praying I have no broken bones. The rips in my brain don't heal. There's a larger tear each time. They stop me from feeling.

Uncle came and found me, said he was worried I didn't come down to help him. He looked at me and he knew. He kept shaking his head, looking at the floor. He looked angry; I have never seen him like that. I couldn't stop telling him I was sorry. He cried. Still I could not feel. That was the worst thing.

Leah is light-headed. She doesn't recall coyote attacks, she has a terrible feeling something beyond those words happened. Trying to remember, she takes extra-strength painkillers.

NAVAJO RIVER, Verse Two

There's a mystery here I cannot understand
Messages and signs that came when I was sleeping
The song you sing echoes across the river
And is carried by the birds far above
There's a band of turquoise reaching between us a colour very old
I see this colour when I think of you
Standing in that river alone
I see you standing in the river of love
I see you calling me to you I see your long hair flowing
And I see you standing in that river alone.

Leah reads an entry she has made in her new journal. These are not her words. Her stomach lurches as she understands whose words these are.

Don't play with fire. It's powerful. It can hurt you. I told you that. And I died by fire. Sammy was tryin' to wake me up. They found him kneelin' beside my bed. They say he looked like he was prayin'. Maybe he was.

I laughed a lot. I liked Player's cigarettes, beer, and women that weren't Indian. I joked when people criticized my life, "Hey, I'm here for a good time, not a long time." I was right. So I'm glad I smoked so many cigarettes, drank so much beer, had so many women, and got into fights when I was drunk.

Now I have no cigarettes, no women, no beer. Nobody sent any over for me. I try to talk to those livin' and ask, but they don't hear me. Too busy worryin. They can't hear. Me, I never worried; just laughed and fooled around.

Called myself "Sundance Kid." Got that from a movie. Didn't know it was a sacred ceremony. I was alive when CB radios were cool. That was my CB name. Sundance. They called it a "handle." Didn't have an Indian name, but I had a CB name.

Talked on that CB when I worked way up on the Dempster Highway. I surveyed that road people drive. All the way to Inuvik. We signed our name on the survival-shack walls, all us road crew. My cousin Lorna found it after I was dead, and she cried. She didn't remember I worked up here until she saw my name. I was behind her yelling, "Hey, Cuz – it's me, Johnnie!" And she didn't hear me when I said I loved her and please not to cry.

I was a city Indian. We called the real Indians "Stick Indians" when they called us "Cities." It hurt, so we had to call them a name back.

I liked that they knew Indian stuff and it bugged me I didn't. My bush cousin Haywire taught me to track my City cousin from bar to bar in Whitehorse. It impressed the white women. He taught me to memorize his boot tracks in the snow and follow them. It was tough in the city, where so many boots walked over those tracks. But it was like Sammy knew, and just when I'd lose his trail he'd walk off the sidewalk into unmarked snow and there I'd catch his trail again. 'Course he could have been staggering, too.

☙

Us cousins were close – the Cities and the Sticks. Sammy and I died together. He coulda got out. Couldn't let me go alone, I guess. But the cousins left behind still have a hard time.

We used to protect each other's girlfriends. I remember Haywire – he's a Stick – went to jail for the winter. We looked out over his girl-friend – maybe a little too much.

We fooled around some but after he got out and got mad, he got mad at her – not me. He never got mad at me. He only said, "Well, at least I know whose hands were on her."

When we drank we would say how much we loved each other. That we were like brothers. Then we'd start fighting – beat each other up bad. Wreck whatever place we were in. The next day we'd wake up stinkin' of booze with it coming right out our skin. We'd see each other's black eyes and laugh. Those bruises told the story we couldn't remember.

☙

Leah was confused. Haywire had gone to jail? She had fooled around with Johnnie? No! This cannot be true! Her head pounded, and her throat ached.

☙

That Stick, he still hunts, still runs fish nets. He still knows the old stories. Now he's a father and is teaching those little ones. I didn't even have a kid. Least not one anyone told me about. I knew nothing about

117

my culture except one song – a Tlingit song, from my dad. It was about bein' homesick and longing to go back to your home country.

Once, some of the boys and I were in a bar in Alaska. Cousin Stick called me City. Said I knew nothing about being an Indian. I stood right up in that bar and sang that Indian song. Everybody stopped talking and listened, even the white people. And I sang real loud. The Stick's mouth was wide open. He didn't know even one song.

An old Tlingit guy came up and asked, "Who's your mother?" That's their way of placing you. I told him he wouldn't know her – she was Southern Tuchone, from the Yukon. But then I said who my dad was. He knew our family was one of the coastal Tlingit ones who long, long time ago went overland into the Yukon and stayed.

That trip, we sat around a fire on the beach with that old man. He got crabs and put them on the fire, alive. They kept walkin' out, he kept throwin' 'em back.

He teased us, that old guy, said, "You Yukoners gotta chase game all through the mountains to get something to eat. We just pick our food right out of the water."

I said, "Yeah, but when we put our food on the fire, it don't walk out of it!" Boy, we busted a gut. And I knew it didn't matter I didn't grow up there. Those people were my relatives, and they felt it too. It was the way we laughed together over that joke. Like we were hugging in a mountain pass after not seein' each other in a hundred years.

❧

March, 1994
I'd like to meet the Old Ones from long ago. I bet they were earthy, real, gritty, and had some Medicine People humour amongst themselves. Like emergency-room humour. Uncle still looks serious, between laughs.

People who are practising ceremony now are like Catholics and Protestants. Or they're every kind of religion. The "every kind of

religion" Indians are ceremony junkies. Those who go to every heal-
ing circle, sweat lodge, potlatch, Big House gathering, or healing cer-
emony they can get their desperate mitts on. Worse, there are those
who run every kind of ceremony imaginable. Experts in them all.
Uncle says I have a funny way of looking at things. He did finally
start smiling again. It was hard to see no smile. I wonder what is up
with him?

Q?

A strange cry launches Leah out of deep sleep, surfacing from
deep water. She shoves flattened hair from her face, feels tears on
her cheeks. Disoriented, drunk from lack of sleep.

"Not again," she sobs. She needs to see the time. Why is it
3:00 a.m.?

Breathing deep, she fights to sit up. She pulls her long hair
back and holds it off her neck to cool her skin.

By moonlight she finds her journal on the table. What mat-
ters now is to write or this dream it will possess her for days. The
words move across the page as she tries to render the dream story.
Sammy's story. She still hears his voice.

Why are all these people from the other side talking to her?
Sobs surge and overtake her. *Why?* She howls, her face deep in
her pillow hoping she cannot be heard.

Q?

My name is all my parents gave me. I grew up with my brothers and
sisters in Whitehorse. Our foster parents were white. And Catholic.
That was okay. Except they didn't like Ind'ns. At least us kids had each
other. There was seven of us. We looked out for each other.

119

When I was fifteen, I went to party on the riverbank. Cops couldn't see us there, 'cause it slopes down to the Yukon River. There was this smartass guy there, and he was pissing me off. "Who does this guy think he is, anyways?" I said to the guy next to me. He said, "Oh, that's Johnnie, we call him "Dean Martin" because he's so entertaining." Then he burst out laughing, and I got that he was being a smartass.

Later I found out Johnnie was my cousin. I never had a cousin before. I liked the guy. Once I got him over thinking he was the coolest guy around, he was the coolest guy around.

I started hangin' around Johnnie every day. Him and I, we got along good. I had a better time because he knew different Ind'ns.

He used to call my girlfriend the A&W Rootbear. That's because she was big like that bear and she worked at the A&W when it was open in summer. Maggie the Rootbear, he called her. Yeah, that and her uniform was just what that bear was wearin'. Every time we were watching TV and that commercial came on, with that Rootbear waddlin' his fat ass around, he'd start laughing with a smartass grin and say, "Hey, look, Sammy! It's Maggie!" Man, he never got sick of laughing at that Rootbear.

Once, he got me real good. We had a couple of bucks. We were hungry. Went to Dixie Lee Fried Chicken. There weren't too many places open in the winter up here.

I got a joke. "Hey, how do you know you're in Whitehorse in August? Easy, because the Dairy Queen is closing down for the winter." Why that's funny? Thing is, it use ta!

So, there we were. We ordered and got two chicken dinners to share. We see our country cousin Haywire walkin' up, and Johnnie runs out and gets him. Geez, it was weird how Arthur would just show up like that, when he came into town from the bush like he knew where to find us!

Anyways, I went to the can. Meanwhile I didn't know those guys had moved tables. This white family took our first table. Well, how was

I supposed to know? I wanted to scare those idiots, and so I jumped out from behind the divider and raised my arms up like a bear and yelled as loud as I could, "YAH!" like an Indian war cry in a Western. Only it wasn't my cousins, it was that white family and they went whiter, and the dad dropped his chicken. My cousins snickered at the next table. They told me later I kinda stood there with my arms up like a bear for a while, and went real white – well, I'm pretty dark, so as white as I could go.

Geez, I felt stupid. And that white family thought I was nuts. A drunk. I could tell. They kept looking over real scared the whole time we were there. Their little girl had big eyes and they stayed on me. I couldn't wait to get out of there. Johnnie and kept breakin' out snickerin' the whole time we were in there, lookin' at each other and shakin' their heads. Geez, I coulda choked the both of 'em!

Johnnie and Haywire had real nice cowboy boots. Me, I had winter boots for cold weather. Didn't figure I was the cowboy boot typa guy.

They always bugged me: They said I didn't need shiny cowboy boots, because everyone was lookin' at my shiny smile like I didn't know how to do anything else.

Haywire's girlfriend Leah said I had a smile that could light up the world. I thought that was how her smile was.

Man, we were all in love with that girl. She didn't even know it. When I tried to tell her one day she just said, "Sammy, I don't wanna hear about it!" I just wanted her to know she was special to us. She wasn't from us, but she was part of us. Wish I got to tell her that. But, after I died, and saw how hard she cried at the funeral, I knew she felt it.

Yeah, I died way before I meant to. I didn't get to see my nieces and nephews grow up. I didn't get to see the next spring, and the wild roses that grow all over up on Grey Mountain. That's where they planted me.

Johnnie got buried up in his mom's village, 'cause up here we follow our mom's way. Me, I didn't follow anyone, nobody remembered where Mom was from. I had a Catholic funeral.

An old drunk man thought the priest was takin' too long. He started yellin' at the top of his lungs right in the church, "Let's get this show on the road!"

But you know what? I got a fancy gravestone. Johnnie got a tent, because his family didn't have the money to put a grave house around him. Some people get 'em with windows and everything. Some just get a fence, just around the grave. I guess so they won't wander out of the graveyard after. Johnnie's Mom and Dad stayed with his body for four days and nights. That's the old way.

They had a Anglican funeral, I guess for insurance. The minister sang hymns to a cassette in a fallin' down log church. Real off-key.

They threw Johnnie a potlatch after. Yup, I saw where they stuck up a grave tent in that little Indian village graveyard above the river over my cousin's mom's village.

All my friends came to send me off. You shoulda seen all the cars! They didn't pour a twenty-sixer of C.C. on my grave like I always told them to if anything happened. But Leah is gonna do it one day. She remembered, and she keeps thinkin' about it and it's a lotta years ago! I see that when I hang around her at night.

One night, four years after the fire, she prayed for all of us that died. We were there waiting. Smiling at her in a circle around her bed when she woke. She stared at us, smiling back, until she remembered we were dead. She freaked right out. We had to leave because her mind couldn't take it, us being there. Oh well, least she knew we came to visit. And I got to see her smile one more time before she hollered, "Holy Sheee-IT" – at the top of her lungs.

I won't say anything else, but that girl doesn't wear anything when she sleeps, heh heh.

Leah woke, panicked, as she remembered – she had no job.

She picked up the journal and read, recognized nothing. The handwriting didn't look like hers. These were not her words. They were those of Haywire's cousin Sammy. She could not read past the first lines. She went back to bed and did not wake up until Sunday.

CHAPTER SIXTEEN

MOON OF THE WITCH, Verse Three

Wake up sudden
Someone screaming my name
Can't hear nothing
Oh, but I heard it just the same
Straight to the heart
It ain't no wonder I'm so afraid of the dark

Chorus:
Can't sleep under that moon, no
Can't sleep under that moon
Oh no no, oh no, no, no, no, no, no

❧

Faro Festival CBC Sunday Night Concert
The workshops yesterday went good and I had a good performance last
night. I got laryngitis today. I went into the gym and deep-breathed.
*   I was croaking like a frog when I talked about the songs, but when*
I sang my voice was right there! It was so amazing to hear my name
announced just before I walked on. To be up on that stage, blinded by
lights, seeing only the first two rows of people. Knowing there were hun-
dreds. Feeling their pride because I was representing the Yukon. I swear
their applause for the Northern performers was much louder.

My knees could easily have given out. I was so overwhelmed by nerves! But I did it. I focused on Uncle right in the front row. He was smiling up at me, and he stood right up and clapped hard after every song. I surprised him when I sang the one I wrote for him, "Courage in my Eyes." I could see tears in his eyes.

When I went up to the performers lounge right after playing, the famous performers gave me a standing ovation! I was so amazed. Humbled. I never expected that.

Bruce Cockburn leaned over and said, "We do that when we recognize ones who will be coming up now."

I couldn't say a word. I could only smile. I feel so over the moon! I can't sleep and it's 1:00 a.m.

♥

Monday Morning!
Uncle and I are on the bus home. There's so much to write, but I'm feeling really tired after a jam-packed weekend. One of the professional backup musicians just walked down the bus to give me his business card! He said when I'm ready to record I should come to Edmonton and I can stay with him; he would arrange whatever I need. Uncle Angus just looked at him, dead straight. Not smiling. That's not like Uncle, he is usually pretty friendly. Then I understood that this guy was trying to take advantage and had bad intent. I just thanked him and took it as a compliment. I could tell Uncle was not happy with him. He was looking at him very seriously, and the guy got nervous, couldn't finish his sentence, and went back to his seat.

My performance went fantastic and the workshops as well. When I made mistakes in the guitar playing, I made them consistently each time around, so they became part of the song. And I'm happy I proved to myself that I can control my voice when I'm very nervous.

I found that I can immerse into the songs. I can feel them as I'm singing. I try so hard to feel what I sing. Even if I'm covering someone else's song, I try to relive whatever the song is about. I try to sing from the pain, or the joy, or the peace the words speak of.

One of the other Yukon performers came up saying something in my voice had touched her deeply and made her cry. I think that's the best compliment I ever had.

I also found out I can forget the words to my own songs, but never covers! That is so totally weird! I have to figure the answer out, because I forgot some lyrics. I just played an instrumental break, let my mind go blank, and the words kind of popped in. I have to work harder to remember the lines. It's a terrible feeling to suddenly go blank.

I also had this strange, mystic thing happen. A couple of times, I went someplace else. My soul travelled while I was singing. I would land back into my body and think, "Oh no, where am I in the song?" But I'd let my instinct tell me, and let it grasp the words. Somehow, I knew I did right.

Q?

The fog world is an ugly stranger. Each morning she awakes to the dense grey that owns everything. Slowly, an angry sun burns through, and for a few hours the sun is high and bright in a deep blue sky. Feeble hope returns. The water sparkles, she can see the mountains. Still, she cannot gather courage to go outside.

By late afternoon fog slinks across the water. It comes slow at first, encroaching just above the sparkling sun water. Then large and swallowing, it sucks Leah's frail hope with it. Each day, this awful swallowing.

Q?

Leah loaded the film labelled "Haywire." She saw his young face on the screen, and a pang went right through her body at the sight of the man she loved so terribly, even now. His wiry frame bent as he hefted a big truck tire toward the open, gaping teeth of the lug nuts.

She heard her voice, off camera, "Tell me about your childhood."

❦

"Don't interrup – I gotta get these new moggasins on my truck. Geez, good thing these tires are the same big.

"So, like I said, I don't know who my dad was. My mother you know is Doris from the Charlie family, from Little Annie Lake. I grew up at the lake, with Mom, all my uncles and aunties, and Gramma Maisey. Great Gramma went last springtime; she was 102. We knew when she told us all one day, 'Don't cry for me when I'm gone.' All the old people use ta warn us like that. It made us scared 'cause we knew it meant they were gonna go, and they were always right.

"We all lived in the log cabin my Great Grandpa built, by the lake. I don't remember much about him, 'cept that everybody respected him and listened to him, and nobody acted disrespectful around him."

"What was the worst thing that ever happened?" her younger voice asked. Why would she have asked him such a thing?

"When I was six, the RCMP came and grabbed me for the Anglican Mission School for Indians in Carcross. That place was bad. Fed us mouldy food, most of it had maggots. We knew not to eat those things. I threw it up mostly. They locked us in rooms for days if they didn't like how we behaved.

"My cousin Molly never said I was her cousin, or they wouldn't have allowed us to talk. She tried to watch over me. I never forgot that.

Anyways, I kept takin' a group of little kids through the mountains away from that school. Some kids weren't bush trained, so I found food for 'em. Roots, berries, the inside bark of trees we could eat, even in winter, if I couldn't snare rabbits. We always got caught and sent back.

"Once, it was by an RCMP. He asked us about why we ran away. He took us back, and in front of the whole school he said he wanted to eat with us kids. I remember that Head Matron looked real worried. 'No, come and eat in the staff room,' and he says, 'No, feed me what you made for these kids' – and that cop sat right down with us. After that, things changed lots. I think that cop musta said something and it made things a little better. They never had maggots in the food and nobody got beaten into the dirt after that. Not in front of anyone, anyways.

"That bad nighttime stuff still happened. I know.

"I grew up huntin' before I went off to that school. Knew how to trap, snowshoe the trapline, and ice-fish. We gaffed round fish in the fall, in the creek near the cabin. Had to be careful, there was wolverines there.

"One time I came on a wolverine on the path to the road. That wolverine stood up like a human and put his paws out to me just like he was tellin' me to stop. Then I smelled the grizzly. Man, they stink! That wolverine was tryin' to warn me about the grizzly just up the trail. Good thing I listened.

"The animals on this lan' can tell you a lot. Like every time somebody close to me dies, before I hear about it there's something that I see. They're not real shy, unless you have a dog in your yard. One time I caught one standing in the bush near the house. It wasn't afraid of me. But if three people die on the same night, like in the fire I lost my cousins Johnnie and Sammy, and Sammy's girl, three of them were there just on the side of the road when I was driving. They just stood there together. It happens every time."

"How come you go and get your mom when you knock down a moose?" Leah heard laughter in her younger voice.

"I'm a good hunter, but I go grab my mom when I got something. I don't look Indian to some people, so I used to get 'Dry Meat' – my nickname for dark-skinned Indian – so the Game Warder wouldn't give me no trouble. Must look like the old man; he musta been some white guy. I look for him sometimes on the street, when I go to town. Try to see if some guy looks like me.

"Don't like town, me, I like the bush. Use ta like visitin' Gramma up the road, with Uncle Angus, he looked after her. The band made a new house for them and put it up on a hill. Only thing is, the water ran down the hill so the outhouse ran into the creek.

"Remember when Gramma got real sick and spent five months in the Whitehorse hospital? Geez, when you and me picked her up she got ready to go in five minutes, her kerchief and all! I remember how happy you and I were. She wanted to stop by the bead store, and next thing I knew – $150 of my bucks later – she comes out, me hauling bags of beads, hides, needles. Man, all she wanted to do was get home and sew and bead! She called me Grandsonny. I never saw her so happy!

"Remember when I teased her about she had to pay me back, she pointed her finger at me an' said, 'Shit you!' just like she always did. You and I grinned at each other. Tried hard not to laugh"

❧

In the film labelled "Gramma Maisey," Leah watches Gramma's tiny hands flicker on the screen, illustrating the story as she speaks. Leah loves how she drawls the vowels for emphasis:

"I been born lo-o-ong time ago. Been same place a-a-all my life. Hard growin' up time. Go hunting lo-o-ong ways, stop, dry meat. Run fish nets wintertime. Haul moose quarter on my back. Haul water. Lo-o-ots hard work. Oh, boy. Never stop. Hands cold runnin' nets under ice

wintertime. We work hard that time. Sometime real cold, no food, animals quit movin', can't hunt. One winter no food – ate spruce tree, inside part. Boy, re-e-eal happy when we got moose that time.

"*My mom, she die when I only eleven year 'ole. I do her jobs. Lo-o-ots hard work, feed kids, make clothes, clean clothes, lots work. Thirteen kids. No friends. No time. Too much to do, too far in bush. Travel to town once year maybe. Carcross. See Kutchen people that time. White people. They don' like us. Say we stink. We say they the stink thing. We bath in snow water that time. Ruuuub down hide clothes and moccasins with fresh snow wintertime. Summertime swim in lake.*

"*I like swim that time, me. I swim re-e-eal good.*

"*Sad when baby die springtime right after mom go. My father quit talkin' lo-o-ong time that time. Baby sick, no money for medicine. Hard for Ind'n people that time – lo-o-ots babies die, we call 'em 'Baby' first two years. They only get name after, 'cause so many die.*

"*Never get shoe 'til grown. Wear moggasins. Make for all my brothers and sisters and father. Jacket sometime too, with beadwork if we got money for beads.*

"*Ha-a-ard get money that time. Only from sellin' trapline furs that time. When I was twelve, me an' my brother trapped furs as high as a .22 – that how much it cost for our own .22 that time.*

"*U.S. Army come Second Worl' war, make pipeline all that way Norman Wells, Dad cousin lead 'em through bush on dog team that time.*

"*First time I see Negro man, no woman. They like Indian girls and lo-o-ots have babies. Nobody care. Lo-o-ots Ind'ns die that time, got sick from those army people. Lots babies die, they happy for new ones. And some army man they don't ask for be with Ind'n women, just do it. Not Negro ones, they like be with Ind'ns, they laugh same like us. They always come visit. Bring food for kids. They been good to us Ind'ns. Some stay with Ind'n woman when army gone. Got lo-o-ots kids.*

"That time we travel by raft summertime, love dog team winter-time. Snow come, dogs go from pack dog to sleigh dog. They love sleigh. Hard work, cook feed for dogs. Bear dog we got to keep bears away. Pack dogs for heavy carrying. Bi-i-ig pot on fire outside, I do that time. One time dogs bit from no food. Arm got real sick. Father got spruce pitch, mix up with bear grease. Make that sickness go that time. Oh, boy, that hurts. Haul water for family sore arms. Bath those kids with sore arm, haul wood with that sore arm.

"Real tough for Ind'ns that time. Not like people with truck and those skidoo. Us we just got dogs, our feet, raft, sleigh.

"Boy, those times we work hard all day from sun come up and sun go down. We know sign – bush sign. When to hunt, when moose com-ing down from high country fall time. Know when best berry pickin'. Boy, us girls we like berry pickin'. No boys, just girls and we la-a-augh and la-a-augh and tell stories."

Leah's chest ached as tears streamed. The voice on the film caressed her heart like Gramma's tiny hands.

"That time we don't talk to men – only brothers, fathers and uncles and cousins. Bad if we look at man. Never do. Keep eyes down. Old way my mother taught me.

"I know best rabbit snare. We watch animals to know best place snare, catch lots. They fight and waiting when we come by and run those snares. Lo-o-ots times we could only eat those rabbits and they kept us alive.

"If we look at men in eyes, we could snare like rabbits but Mother wants good girls, so we listen, but laugh about set snares for men.

"Sometime coyotes steal our snare game. Those coyotes come after our dog, but bear dog they bark, and scare 'em off. Grouse too, we get without .22, all you need is good aim an' a rock. Hit 'em in the head. Same way porcupine – we club 'em, singe 'em. We dry lots fish, meat for wintertime; gee, lots work for us. Fall time, tan hides with brains –

*hides re-e-eal soft. Put rabbit fur inside winter moggasin, those made
high up so snow don't get in. Keep foot warm better than any boot.*

*"Sure like Grandsonny, Arthur, bring me rabbit and grouse all
time. He think of Gramma first all time. I keep bannock and tea on
stove, he always hungry, that Arthur.*

*"Husband Jimmy, meet him first at uncle's house, I am thirteen.
Came lo-o-o-ong way – Alaska. Re-e-eal handsome. I like he smile but
not look at him, feel that smile on me. Not too long he ask Father to
marry me. I glad, already thinking to marry but girl can't ask.*

*"We stay there with Father, look after small kids yet 'til grown, no
girls to do it, gotta hunt and dry meat and fish. When the kids grown
enough we build log house, him and I happy by lake over a ways... but
he die. I got eighteen kids that time.*

*"Brothers came help me for food all time. Good family help like that
old time. Kids die too, get sick; we cook our medicine, but I don't know
medicine for that new sickness and some die. Lots die before ever get old
enough for name. I got ole, me.*

*"Hard lose babies, kids. Over next life we got big family, lots kids.
One day be all together. Even young die these days. Lots leave too early.
Make big family for them there, small for us here. Used to be other way.
Hard life for them now, all weather warm and no old signs to go by to
live old way."*

✑

WAITING FOR THE GRACE TO FALL, *Verse Two*

*Can you not see it's all in you?
My words will only distract, confuse you
It's all within and that's the truth
No one can find for you but you*

I'm watching without watching
Like the Old Ones do, watching
Just watching for the grace to fall
Just watching for the grace to fall

ॐ

Leah finally sleeps. She is home. The road walks ahead, an old friend with gravel feet. She follows. Her blood, skin, bones, walk through timeless scape. She knows this place, she is unafraid.

Snow spiral-dances. She raises her face to a deep, deep dark sky that touches down to the earth. The silence. She has forgotten about this deep silence. Between her feet the road snow creaks, a call and response.

Lightning flashes the land from black to day, from black to day, from black to day. Mountains crouch, leap, vanish again, leap forward, hide back, leap forward, hide back. Snow-dusted spruce trees appear, disappear, appear, disappear again. Something, something…creeps, spider-walks from within her bones out to skin. She will not allow fear to creep, to leer, to taunt, to clown. The spider walking on her scalp drums the silence away with hard beats. She speaks her name aloud – first softly, then a desperate cry. She calls out in the only three words of the language of this land she knows. "Lightning Medicine Woman, Lightning Medicine Woman, Lightning Medicine Woman." The mountains toss her name back – echo, echo, echo. "Medicine Woman …Medicine Woman…Medicine Woman." In this way she prays. There is something, someone, just beyond. As the land is lit yet again, the Other Side people; she knows their names. She wills spider to spirit-dance, lightning held in its jaws, from her skin into the marrow of her bones.

She is within the next flash of light. Falls to her knees, blood to stone. Failing light shrouds, lulls. She surrenders into a tranquil black.

She wakes. Jangling in her ears, heart thundering. Shaken to the deep. Stupefied. Hunted. It feels as though she has been fighting for her life, death near, waiting in the shadows. Breath catching. This dream shadows, stalks. From dawn she sits watching out the window until the sun crosses the sky and sets, and darkness blankets. Still, she sits. Knowing, like the words to a forgotten song, dances just outside of the grasp of her understanding.

ᖇᖇ

Far away up North, Coyote sniffs the air. Jogs through the meadows. Nothing is moving today. The ground is hard, frozen. A rabbit. Frozen to the spot. He pretends not to see it and lifts his leg on a tree. Rabbit lowers its head to feed. Coyote leaps, wheels, rebounds, lands. Teeth plunge into neck. Coyote plays with this easy kill. Release. Rabbit, heart racing, head down, ears back, hops frenetically, zagging this way, zigging that, feigning left, turning right.

Coyote leaps again and lands the animal. Stands motionless on it for a moment. The rabbit squirms and fights, back paws beating a rapid staccato. Coyote lifts his paw. Free! He catches and releases until she drops from exhaustion.

Coyote tears into her fur. She spasms uncontrollably. He devours until there is nothing but the bloody pelt. He lies in the weak-tea sun, warming and cleaning himself. Grouse. Eyes on the target, the bird eats and ducks its head as it moves. He creeps forward, catlike. Follows, stomach driving him on. He knows this prey will fly, so injures the wings on the first pounce.

The grouse, wings splayed, desperately tries to escape. Coyote takes his time again, chasing, pouncing, chasing, pouncing. Bored now, he rips off the head with a tearing sound. With his paws he holds the bloodied neck, rips off feathers to get to meat. He opens the animal. Pale yellow innards steam in frigid air. He licks and eats, leaving the variegated feathers in a pile where they fall.

❧

In a dream, Leah follows the road to Gramma Maisey's house. Raises her hand to knock at the familiar door. She hears voices. Instead, she listens. An unfamiliar voice. She knows, as one does in dreams, it belongs to Great Gramma Sophie.

"When I get buried, Carcross, big potlatch. Can't believe got 102 years; they say that time. Big party. I been there. They cry at grave, laugh at party. Party for my good husband. Me, too. He been there, too. Eat that plate they burn up. My, they send over lo-o-o-ots wild game. Sweets, too. Moose guts, beaver, porcupine. All kind things they send over. Good to eat, that food.

"My elders come, too. Eat with us. See people stop cry. Smile again. Those family smile know they see me one day again, too. I only sad that Leah did not know us."

Leah stands outside the cabin. She is dirty. Too ashamed to enter. Slowly, head hanging, heart heavy as mountain rock in her chest, she walks back down the road away from the voices. The heaviness does not lift when she opens her eyes.

Chapter Seventeen

Leah's heart fires staccato-like rifles on a range. Deep breath. The second-last diary entry. She cannot look yet cannot turn away. Afraid to read the last of the journal for some days, at last she has found her courage. No date. She has to read it time and time again; she cannot grasp the truth that lies naked and bleeding and alone on that page.

❧

I was putting the rope around my neck. Doris came home. She yelled, ran to me. She is different toward me now. She has never been kind, and now she has been taking care of me.

Doris rushed out when Haywire arrived home from camp. She intercepted him before he came in. I know she told him about the rope, and, somehow, she knew about Coyote. How?

They were outside still. I saw Coyote above her head, so I knew she was talking about him. Haywire cried in her arms for a long time. Doris cried with him.

I watched from the window and wanted to cry. There is ice inside me. I know my heart is broken, yet I feel nothing.

❧

WAITING FOR THE GRACE TO FALL, *Verse Four*

I'm waiting without waiting
And I'm listening without listening
And I'm watching without watching
And I'm standing with the angels
And I'm being without being
And I'm knowing without knowing
And my eyes are on the heavens
And my feet are on the ground
And I'm hoping without hoping
And I'm knowing without knowing
And I'm waiting for the grace to fall

❧

So much trouble. I sleep all the time. So tired. Haywire drinks a lot more. He goes out of the truck a lot when we are down the lake. I caught him this time, he had a bottle in the back of the truck. After that, he started drinking openly. What do I do now? After Dad, I swore I would never get with a guy who has a drinking problem. This guy has a problem. And I love him. Terribly much.

❧

She drops the diary, filled with dread. With shaking hands, she dials the phone. No answer. The outgoing message.

"Haywire, I need to talk to you." She breaks down. "Haywire, please, it's important."

With her heart in her mouth, choking her so she has to cough, her breath coming fast, she reads the very last entry in the old diary. Fear clangs a cacophony in her ears like a metal alarm, grips her with cruel claws.

More treasure. But we won't have to bury it this time. Haywire says he will look after it for me. I have to go to the hospital in Vancouver. I don't want to, but they say I have to.

Leah is violently ill. Feebly cleaning it up when the phone rings, she runs to get it.

"Leah, what's wrong?"

"God, Haywire, what the hell took you so long to call back?" She hears the tone of hysteria in her own voice. She is more frightened by the tone of his. Her heartbeat comes harder, faster, rattles in her ribs.

"I was up the river. Chaos, what the hell is wrong?"

"I tried to kill myself."

Silence. She hears the fear and love in his voice.

"Again? Leah is there someone that can get to you?"

"No. I mean, at Little Annie. I read it in the diary. Geesuz, Haywire, what the hell happened? Why would I try to take my life? (I didn't remember until I read it). Your mom saved me!"

"Chaos listen to me. Things happened. You weren't yourself. We can't talk about this on the phone. Come back North. We'll talk in person. But we'll need some time."

"Okay, Haywire, maybe I'm not ready to know what happened, yet. I just couldn't believe it when I read it."

"Leah, you are one of the toughest women I know. You made Mom look like Tinkerbell."

Leah feels inner laughter through tears at the thought of a chubby brown Tinkerbell, in a kerchief with a plaid jacket and Elmer Fudd boots.

"I know, Haywire, but I don't remember anything about coming back to Vancouver."

"Don't worry about it for now. It's just a story. And I will tell you when I see you. You gonna be okay?"

"After a big glass of Fireball, maybe!"

"Oh, geez – I don't drink anymore. I had a big argument with booze one night and lost."

She laughs, she can't help it.

"God, Haywire, even now, you can make me feel better."

"Okay, woman, just go easy on the firewater."

"I won't." It's his turn to laugh.

When she puts down her phone, Leah is horrified to find that she has wet herself.

ॐ

Dawn is spreading its fingers across the sky. Her stomach is queasy.

Coffee. Campfire coffee. A can on the stove? No. It was spring water and the fire that made that magic. And the long-gone hands of Uncle Angus.

The telephone officiously interrupts. Something. The ring is different, hopeful. Fear, love battle within her. Love wins. She *must* answer this time. She snatches it up just before it stops.

"Leah? It's time, girl, Indian up!"

"Oh, my God – Lorna!"

"Yup, and you are coming home!"

"I am?"

"Headstone potlatch in four weeks, kid; we need you there. Uncle's last party."

Without hesitation, Leah hears herself say, "I'll book a flight."

BACK TO THE RIVER

I've got the mud of the Cowichan River on my shoes
And one good way to lose these livin' blues
I got to run back to the river; got to run down to the water
Got to move to the sound of the rhythm;
Got to lose myself, I got to soothe my demons
Got to run

For a long, long time I haven't listened to the voices in my head
But these days I'm trying to remember what it is they said
I got to run back to the river, got to go down listen to the water
Got to move to the rhythm of its dancing
Got to lose myself in the sound of its chanting
Got to run

❧

A dark shadow drapes like sheets over furniture. The fog has been hanging that way all winter. Leah is gripped by anxiety. An enormous, taunting animal roars in her ears. Terrified and paralyzed.

Five times she calls to cancel her flight but stops herself. She knows going will give her what she needs. She also knows the trip will not give her all the answers.

❧

NAVAJO RIVER

I can see you sitting here, the most beautiful man
I'd ever seen
Like a dream smiling at me
Like something slowly·coming
Out of the misty rain
Like fire burning in the night
Turning the black sky to gold
That spirit shining in you
Turned my blood into a river

❧

SOMEONE ELSE IS DRIVING, *Verse Two*

It's not what you don't have, it's what you've got
Why wait to be happy if you're not
Joy is only a choice we make
And happiness is shy when you are afraid
When someone else is driving you can close your eyes
If the sun is shining, you can see your own designs
Pinwheels dancing in a fire-orange sky
When someone else is driving and you close your eyes
Someone else is driving, may as well close your eyes

❧

The snow has come. Coyote leaves his den with quick bounds. Following the human scent into the meadows, it comes and it goes. He picks it up, loses it, picks it up stronger, loses it.

He hates this smell, but there is an alluring something else. Fat.

He searches, ears twitching, eyes alert, head down, until the scent is stronger and there are two sets of tracks in the snow. His eyes catch a glint of steel in a pile of grass and sticks. A frozen rabbit is waiting. He does not sense danger. The sweet, sickening human stench overwhelms him; he gags and sneezes, shaking his head.

The rabbit will fill his tight, hungry stomach. He takes hold of the rabbit and pulls, hears a strange "clink" and drops the animal. The trap has come out from its hiding spot. He looks at this metal thing from all sides. He pulls with more force on the rabbit. Then, setting one paw on a part of the metal chain, with the power of his jaws he manages to pull the rabbit free.

He carries his prize to his den and goes back, he has smelled more. He pulls the prey from each trap – rabbits, squirrels. The first squirrel does not come easily; one foot tears off and stays clamped in the steel teeth.

Coyote likes this kind of hunting in the morning. There is no effort. He will come back here each dawn to take this food.

He moves all the frozen animals into his den, where they will soften slowly with the heat of his body. He does not wait but grasps a rabbit. He rips away the fur, leaving the remains where they fall.

After a few days, this ripens; but, to Coyote, the smell is delicious. A coyote can never have enough.

☙

Leah woke in the dark. Something had disturbed her sleep. All her senses were straining. The cabin was completely dark.

She caught a familiar skunky scent. Her scalp prickled.

She heard snorting now, and something rubbing up against the logs right by her head. She willed herself not to move. She lay perfectly still.

She could hear and feel movement from her side of the cabin, to the front, and now to the side where the door was. A bear could come in, bolted door or not. She lay waiting. There was nothing to be done.

She wanted to yell out, but knew she must remain soundless. Finally, silence. She breathed easier. She sat up. The cot springs squealed.

She rose, stretched, carefully crossed to the door for a drink of water, lay back down.

She woke gently with the delicious feeling of her body coming awake naturally, without an alarm. She liked the rare times she woke up when her body was ready. She lay still, her eyes closed. Buried herself further into the covers, away from the chilled air. She lay as long as she could.

She rose to make fire. There was the beloved old coffeepot of Uncle's on the shelf above the old stove. How many times had his old hands poured her a cup from the pot? She imagined his fine hands preparing that wonderful coffee he used to share with anyone who dropped in.

She took a long drink from the water dipper, poured water into the pot. Foraged for coffee in the box by the door, and the small container of cream.

She looked out the window to the lake. It was perfectly still. The mountains, snow dusted, were perfectly mirrored. They spoke to a place deep within her. Reminded her that she had history here. Her DNA was still all over this land. For the first time in months, the inner blood-and-guts whorl finally slowed, stilled.

Her mind was as clear as the panorama before her. She allowed herself to fall deeply into the peace. She hoped she could stay there.

❧

DANCE AWAY, Verse Six

We have been witnesses to these sacred days, these fleeting rainbow
  moments
These tearful voicings, the stories of hearts and their longing for
  reunion
And we will be there alone and yet together to see all the people's
  children rise up
To dance away

And now these petal pearls lay at our feet, behind us, beside us,
On our right, on our left, below our feet
His chosen petal pearls gathered by the winds of His grace
You made me promise never to say goodbye, so I'll just dance away
You made me promise never to say goodbye, so I'll just dance away
Yeah, we don't have to say goodbye, we can just dance away
We can dance away, dance away, dance away.

❧

The night before the potlatch she lapsed into a heavy sleep. Found herself within one of those dreams where she thought she was awake. She heard footsteps outside the cabin, heard the door open. She knew those footsteps. She sat bolt upright.

 "UNCLE"! she yelled, filled with joy.

He was smiling, sat down on the end of the cot. It gave an agonized protest.

"Leah. Last time I saw you was in a dream. I was just so happy to see you – it jumped up in me like a fish. From my feet to my head. Moved in me like how the creek looks when the fish are running. When you drop a gaff in there you get five at once. That was the one only time I saw you without Arthur. It didn't matter. You still hugged me, crying and smiling, same time. Good to see you smile.

"I saw you got sadness way back in your eyes. You pushed it out of the way to have the happiness to show when you looked at me. I thought about that dream a lot after. And I wished you happiness.

"One day, you'll find it. You call it to you, like some people can call animals or birds. Only you don't know yet. But you will. One time you'll understand what those animals and birds say. You don't know that yet too, but I see that. Always saw that."

She woke and lay immersed in all his words. As murky as her mind was, there was something as clear as the water in the creek up the hill that lay there deep within those words.

ℚ

Miles away out on the land, Coyote chases his favourite meat. Beaver has rushed and dived into the lake, and now comes up far enough away to safely smack, smack-smack-smack its tail on the top of the water. It echoes across the lake where a moose's head swings up.

Coyote won't get into the lake. He has been caught in a river current and knows that can take him; the scent of water speaks of danger.

He picks up another smell, and wheels round to follow it. He weaves in and out, following a small game trail that sharply winds over the moss and through low brush.

The wind shifts.

Now upwind, he does not catch even a whiff of the other creature. He comes snout to snout with it, sneezes as the reeking thing snarls; attacks without hesitation. Coyote leaps, yelps, and tears down the path back in the direction he has come.

Wolverine goes back to her search for grubs under the log she has been pulling apart.

Coyote tears at top speed until he has crossed the entire forest, and into the meadows. It is then he feels the terrible pain and sees his paw is bleeding. He goes into his den, licks the raw wound. The throbbing is terrible now, but he knows to lick it as much as he can.

For weeks he has trouble hunting; becomes sullen, bony, wracked by hunger. He can no longer run as fast as he could before.

Chapter Eighteen

Night had darkened the cabin. Leah lit candles. It was time.

She picked the bundle off her bed. Placed it carefully on the table. Breathed in the fragrance of medicines.

She ran her hand across the hide. It was darkened with age. Covered with delicate designs. Red ochre or, maybe, pipestone. Lightning shooting down from stars and moon to the ground. It was exquisite. Like something one would see in a museum.

She opened it. Many little bundles. She took them one by one, carefully unwrapping each.

A blade of sweetgrass. Old-style coiled tobacco. Sage. Cedar. Roots, and medicines she did not know, and yet were familiar. A little bag of charcoal. A piece in her hand, a flash of energy shot up her spine and back down. She vibrated.

She carefully replaced it, stilled.

A little bundle of stones. She could see how old this was. How carefully kept.

She said a prayer of gratitude.

Placed it all neatly back together, exactly as she had unwrapped it.

She left it on the table. Went to bed.

❧

She was walking in the meadows, a beautiful woman was walking toward her dressed in old buckskin, with lightning designs, like the ones on the old bundle. She looked like a young Gramma Maisey. Leah stopped, watched as the Gramma approached.

"Lightning!"

"Gramma, I have missed you so much." Leah embraced her, weeping. It did not seem odd to use the endearment with a stranger who was not unfamiliar. The grandmother held her out at arm's length.

"Lightning. I have been waiting a long time for you. It is time, now. You know who you are, do not ever be afraid. When you feel fear, say your name. When you are lost, say your name. When you feel you cannot go on, say your name."

Gramma bent and made fire. She heated small rocks in the coals. When they were red hot, she placed the stones in a tightly woven basket of medicine. She made tea. She took it off the flames, poured it into a tightly woven cup.

"Drink this tea, Lightning. This will give you what you need. Nuh," she said as she handed it to Leah.

Leah sipped. It was fragrant. Tasted of berries and herbs. She drank it as it cooled.

She looked at Gramma; she had transformed. She was slim and small and had the longest braid Leah had ever seen.

When she bent to stoke the fire, her braid touched the ground.

She looked up at Leah and said, "Do not cut your hair again; this is where your power is. As your hair grows, so shall your power."

Leah filled with gentle peace. She knew who this was. Lightning Medicine Woman. Gramma Maisey's grandmother. She did not want to leave this woman's presence.

Leah woke, in the still of darkness, still immersed in emotions evoked by the dream.

Wide awake, she felt for the matches on the little stool beside her. Zip, hiss, the candle lit, and she sneezed from the sulphur and the scent of hot wax.

She rose and drew water from the bucket by the door. Filled the coffee pot. Began to gently, carefully examine the small bundles until she found the one she recognized.

She smiled, her heart rose. She made fire.

She sang the prayers that knew themselves and rolled easily from her tongue. She made tea as Gramma had in the dream.

She prepared an offering for Lightning Medicine Woman. Only then did she pour some for herself. The fragrance was familiar, bringing her back within the dream.

Leah felt Gramma's presence, here now. She slowly sipped the medicine tea until the sun rose and lit the lake with pink fire.

ꞯꝰ

Coyote has not gone into the forest since his fight with the wolverine. Now he is hungry for fish, and a tingling tells him the fish are running in the creek he knows, down from the meadows. He runs, limping through the forest near to the lake. He trots down to rushing water, still favouring his sore paw. He raises it and lopes along the best he can.

He jumps straight into the creek. This water he knows is safe enough and, though he hates the smell of it, the hunger wins out. Shivering in the cool, his head goes this way and that, watching the darting fish.

Like lightning, he dips his head, catches one. Throws it far enough away that it will not be able to flip itself back into the water. He catches and tosses, until there is a good pile. Thirsty from the work, he drinks.

He has not seen nor sensed Wolverine, who has quietly been eating the fish.

He sees and yelps his surprise. Angered by the hunger tearing at his belly, he leaps out to chase Wolverine away.

Too late, Wolverine sinks her powerful jaws into his throat and shakes. He feels fear and resignation, as his instinct tells him it is too late to fight.

Helpless as he is flung back and forth, back and forth, the light that has always been in front of his eye's fades.

His body relaxes, he releases to the darkness. He is no more.

❦

Leah walked the trail to the creek. Breathed the exhaled breath of spruce, pine, ripening berries. The breeze gentle on her cheek, the sun warm on her back. She felt part of the silence. She inhaled the exhaled breath of the land, deeply.

She heard a raven pass above, and a squirrel whir its warning.

Reaching the creek, she was amazed that it was a couple of arms lengths across and rushing by. It was no longer possible to straddle it as she once had.

It was then she saw the blood, a small animal that smelled like skunk throwing the red-blond animal to and fro, blood streaming from its fur.

❦

FIRE WITHIN

There's a fire within, sister, there's a fire inside,
It can sanctify you or burn you alive

The fire inside, the fire inside, the fire inside.
Choose to be blind or choose to see,
It's all just a matter of degree.
Fuel it with fear or fuel it with love
Fire within, fire below, fire above.
I see the grace in the shadow
I see the grace in the light
I see the grace in the sorrow
And the grace in the joy
The mystery that lies
In the heart of all that is
Forged am I in pain, cooled am I in weeping
Forged am I in pain, cooled am I in weeping
And here am I, oh here am I, oh here am I
I'm an ocean inside.
The ocean inside of me is uncharted territory
Each island is unnamed
Light upon light, strength upon strength
Joy upon joy, and love upon love
Absolute happiness, pray for this, pray for this, pray for this

ॐ

My heart beats gently here. I am a reflection of this ancient land-
scape, patient, waiting, still. I am back in present time, with these
ancient beings, the stone giants and sky and land below. The crags,
peaks dominate everything, as if the humans are nothing within its
enormity. I am surrounded by these mountains, in every direction
that I look. I watch them, and they watch me. I feel the cooled air
of their snow tops. The rock of their bodies. I breathe as they
breathe; their breath redolent with spruce, fall leaves, snow.

Haywire disturbed her reverie as he rose from his chair. He drew water, drank.

Leah's eyes fell on his hands; the most beautiful hands she had ever seen. Moving sculptures in the late morning light as he poured coffee grounds into the pot. Stoked the fire. Her skin hungered for his touch. Her desire rose. She looked back outside, willing the heat to dissipate. It did not.

She heard the bloop, bloop, bloop of water boiling. The fragrance of tea reaching her where she sat.

Her want spoke with a forgotten pang in her belly. He sensed her. Turned. His eyes touched hers.

The heavy sweet fragrance of tea mingled with wood smoke. She stood; eyes on his; crossed to him before he willed her to. She put her arms around his neck. There was a knowing.

They slowly kissed. A flame caught pitch on wood and roared in the stove.

The feel of his tongue pulled a moan from her. Louder as the kisses crossed from her lips to her face, down her neck, lower where her shirt was open. She pulled him to the cot.

His weight on her. In his jeans, now shirtless. Her breathing rapid, she buried her face in his neck. Her warm breath opened something within him. Behind his ear she found his familiar scent. She breathed him in and cried out loud.

His face panting breath hot between her breasts, he raised his head, spoke in aching tone, "It's been so long."

"Too long." She could barely speak the words.

"No; I mean for me…this has not been part of my life for a long, long time."

She moaned deep, low. The inside of her felt starved for him. She gripped him low from behind, on his now bare bottom, pulled him closer, hard.

Now he cried aloud, "Leah!"

Sweet curve of her lip; the fragrance of her breath.

Skin to skin. Free. Their old together fire.

He rolled her, and she called out, ecstatic, when he slow-kissed her across her back. She moved as her hand reached down for him, moved down so that her mouth could taste his salt with her tongue. She heard his quick panting as she spoke with tongue and lips to flesh, until he called out loud and begged her to stop.

"Take me inside."

She straddles him and says, "Look at me," as her hand moves to guide him within.

Watching her face for signs, he moves with her. Free-riding like this, the heat of him inside her, her hands grasping him closer still.

They speak in words they barely hear, banshee calling. Head thrown back, hair wild, Leah growls, howls.

A lightning dance, writhing, convulsing, primordial. She feels an ocean within her roil, moil, surge. Ebb, flow. Ecstatic, joy-filled, Leah looks him full in the eyes and moves, the way he remembers, then collapses on him panting hard, wet with exertion.

He waits. Knowing his waiting, she moves to where he lies on his back, looks with eyes of heat and want. With mouth and tongue she tastes and takes the sweet salt of each pulse of him.

They lay entwined, warm.

❧

Wolves – the electrifying song of calling sounds in the deep silence. There is nothing but a flicker of orange-red light from the grate.

He says, "Look what your howling started."

Cathartic, her laughter comes from the same deep place as her sorrow.

Haywire brings her coffee. She sits, smiles, drinks deeply and sighs. It's perfect. And so is he.

She puts the cup down. Still the old fire smoulders.

Now they are slow. This dance different. Hands entwined, they will take their time. She slow-melts, honey, butter, cinnamon drip. Spring thaw; drops flow to creek, to river, thunder of white water. Their old together dance of joy.

She runs her hand on him, then dances fingers over the ripples of granite abdomen. With her tongue she follows Sahara, dune contours.

With her tongue she explores him, between his legs, then higher and he quakes. Afterward, they look at each other full in the eyes. Close eyes now to disappear within. Violet-blue, yellow, green, moving, river of colour behind lids.

He calls her name, *again, again* she moans her response. Call and response, call and response. They explore old territory.

He smiles with lusty, half-open eyes, she sees their fire flicker; she quietly laughs.

With sweet tug of hair, they come together, fall apart, come together, fall apart.

The fragrance of the coffee and smoke on their skin; she implores for his hands, heart, spirit.

He loves her, again. When dawn slow-dances across the sky, she sleeps.

"I am home, Leah; I am home with you," he whispers. Leah stirs and smiles, moves yet closer. Her breath on his chest, a deep sweet pang in his heart.

He holds her with all that he is, her unbearably sweet breath on his cheek as she sleeps.

In the deep of dark, Leah dreams. Cannot wake. This place is too familiar. She knows what is to happen next will be terrible.

She sees, feels the heavy overcast sky rendered white, the trees stark black. Danger. No, no, no! Wake up! Wake up, now!

In the dream Haywire and Coyote are stupid drunk. Leah trembles, outside the cabin, desperate to be somewhere, anywhere else.

Coyote spits, "I can hit anything with one bullet, and I taught you how to shoot."

"No – Gramma never took you in until I was five. I was already bringin' food for her."

Coyote is louder, harsh. His fetid booze stink reaches Leah where she stands. She wants to run.

"*I* taught you how to hunt."

Haywire's voice is harder. "My blood uncles taught me."

Coyote's face reddens. His look is dangerous; she hears him grinding sharp teeth.

Haywire's shoulders go back. Unflinching, he glowers straight into Coyote's eyes, takes one step closer. The click of the safety catch going off on a .30-30.

She tastes fear, like the smell of gunmetal, in her mouth. Coyote turns to her. His eyes at her feet, slowly go up her, stopping at her breasts. She tries to make herself smaller; she feels nausea; sweat trickles between unwashed skin and dirty clothes.

Silent, unmoving, tiny breaths, eyes to the ground, she flickers a glance up at Haywire. Her guts wrench as his eyes narrow and face tightens. His face hard as he stared at her.

Tears start. She has not welcomed Coyote's attention. She bolts like an alarmed rabbit from the two reeling, drunken men.

Behind her, intermittent thunder of two rifles. Something moves on her scalp. She feels something at the back of her head. She hears herself say, "Sorry, Mama, I don't want to die."

She tears open Doris's door, ducks inside. It is only then she reaches up to find her scalp is still intact. She breathes a little when she sees wood chips and sawdust in her hand. She knows it must be from the bullets striking the doorway and leaving chips of wood in her hair.

She cowers inside. There is no place to hide. She cannot fit under the bed. *Oh, my God, they will shoot me, or each other*. She makes herself small, cowering in a corner of Doris's room. Sobbing uncontrollably, she tries to stay quiet.

Door crashing, slamming. Coyote's voice, taunting. "Know what I'm going to do to you? Now your bastard boyfriend is dead, I'm going take what you want to give me, bitch."

His hands on her. A woman screaming. He slaps her hard. His hands are rough on her skin. Terribly familiar.

She tries to wake up. Desperate, trying to get away, to fight. Coyote is stronger, his revolting lust. Rejected by her kicking, thrown into a hurricane force of blind rage, power lust.

His hardness on her stomach goes soft. He raises his fist, she hears it strike. Everything goes black. Now she is a raven. From up high where she flies, she sees Haywire. He is crumpled on the ground. Like a discarded pile of his own clothes.

He cries like a child alone in the world, devastated, betrayed, opened, raw. He knows now who Coyote is. From on high she can see the kicked-puppy look in his eyes.

Now Raven watches. The woman is brave, biting, kicking, scratching. Fighting one more losing fight.

Raven, looking through the window above that woman's head, sits. Fluffing feathers, flit, flash of blue-black, flutter, small jump, cocking of head. The rotten booze breath drips from Coyote's tongue, reaching Raven. His familiar ugly laughter.

The woman on the floor locks eyes with that raven. She looks at that raven so hard she becomes the raven again; when a fist connects with the woman's face, she does not feel it.

Dizziness. The woman sobs. He laughs, a dry, ugly sound. Mocks her, again, tears her shirt wide open. Breasts spill out.

She and the raven fly away. Far, far above the jack pines and spruce. Somewhere below, where the people live, she knows Coyote bruises a woman's breasts. Again. She is a raven, so she does not, cannot feel the pain, feel her nipples hardening from fear, or hear the terrible words whispered in the woman's ear.

"You know you want it." He is moaning, she flies, so she does not hear him unzip his pants; feel his hardness tear into her. Does not feel him biting her skin hard as he rams himself inside her over, and over and over. Does not feel the tearing of flesh, or the blood as it flows again.

As she flies with Raven, something tears and separates in her tiny black head; she knows the man is slamming into a shamed woman, but she soars on a wind far above trees, moss and house soaring in the silence. Knows, but does not feel pain with every ugly driving force of the man far below.

Does not hear Haywire in the distance, his faraway voice screaming, "You bastard, you bastard, Dale Post, I love her! Gramma treated you like a son!"

The woman below hears Haywire shouting, "Leah, no. Leah, I didn't know. I can't walk, my leg is broken, I can't help you." She is hit so hard now that just she succumbs to blackness.

But Leah is flying, free. She hears nothing but the wind in her ears, feels the currents of the cool air in her feathers, on her bird skin as she soars far above the trees. Far from the human sounds, into deep and perfect silence.

Now Leah dreams she is a witness. Doris comes home, Raven is sitting in the corner chair, motionless. Doris immediately demands to know who has been shooting up her house.

The raven woman wonders, *How the hell can Doris see such a tiny hole above the door? How can she see the change in this old shack? How?*

But she has. Haywire says nothing, hangs his head, crying silently. Doris is fierce. She already knows what has taken place.

Haywire, looking like a dog with his tail between his legs for the rest of the day. Despite a broken ankle, he hauls snow for water, cuts enough wood for two weeks, even dumps the reeking, heavy piss pail. Women's work.

Haywire won't look at Raven, who stays unmoving slumped in another corner.

ଐ

Leah woke terrified, stunned, lying in the corner, on the cot, alone. The thin light told her it was late afternoon. She was cold. She remembered she and Haywire had burned all the wood the night before. Careless!

At the chopping block outside, she sensed something dreadful, long before she heard the truck. She stood like stone, watched it run a crazy course down toward her, rising and falling on the bumpy track. It slammed to an abrupt stop. Dale Post. Coyote. He staggered a few steps and dropped. Leah was immobile, disbelieving, unfeeling. He got up, lurched toward her with a leer. She held the axe tightly across her body with two hands.

"Well, Miss Thunder and Lightning," he drawled thickly. She saw and felt his ugliness shrouding her. His small, wild coyote eyes were on her; hard, wet black pebbles in the bottom of a stream.

"How about it if you show me how loud that bed can squeak in there one more time?"

Leah did not say a word, stared unblinking at him. He came toward her. She knew what he wanted.

As if his brain were crystal, she could see his thoughts. He wanted to tie her up. Again. He wanted to beat her. Again. He wanted to do unspeakable things. Again. This time, it would be for many days. Then he was going to slowly kill her. She could see where he had chosen to dump her body, to let the animals have her. High up on the Skagway Road. Down in a gulch. Under the blueberries in the thick moss.

Leah felt stirring in her womb. She raised the axe above her rounded belly as he lurched toward her. Still he did not stop. She turned the blade toward herself.

He was close enough now she could smell the alcohol; see the ugly, hunting, cruel Coyote look she knew only too well.

She hesitated, a dead calm fell over her. It was the only thing left for her to do. She raised the axe, it hung in the air at face level. It was time. She was ready. She swung, hard. She heard it strike but did not feel the blade. She waited for the sense of her blood leaking from her, the weakening. Soon, it would all be over.

She looked straight, fearless, into Coyote's eyes. Saw the light slowly fade. Everything was black. Like a dream, a vision, she then saw herself in slow motion as she turned, buckled, fell like a tree, bouncing slightly. Blood. Her blood like a river, her blood. It was done.

She came to. Haywire's voice.

"Leah, are you are okay? I saw you trying to hit yourself, but you tripped. The axe hit that son of a bitch when you passed out."

She struggled up on her elbow. Saw Dale Post like a bloodied heap of laundry on the ground. The axe embedded in his skull, listing.

She heard an animal scream before she realized it was her voice.

❦

COURAGE IN MY EYES, *Verse Two*

I am walking on an ancient battleground
Asking Simon how can this be
And Simon says the Creator is All powerful All wise
I want to be a warrior with courage in my eyes
I want to be a warrior with courage in my eyes

CHAPTER NINETEEN

Leah woke; struggled for air. Haywire was gone. She was alone. This, then, was the truth. This terrible, ugly thing had happened. All these terrible things she now remembered.

There was more, but this was enough; she willed the other truths away.

A heat came up from her feet to the top of her scalp. She felt as if her blood would boil. Outside. She needed to throw up. Still in her pyjamas, barefoot, she bolted out the door. She vomited right outside in failing light.

She took off up the path in the cold air, heading for anywhere but this place. This place where this thing had happened. She could smell his rank breath. Could not erase the scene that played like a video loop her head.

Dale Post, gushing blood, slowly turning, eyes still looking into hers, bewilderment swallowed by death as his life drained from him. Slow-motion falling, crashing to the ground, bouncing like a tree. Her falling into shrouding darkness. It played over and over, and over.

She had to run; run from this dreadful sight.

Like a panicked animal, she bolted through the woods.

Leaving the path in the blinding dusk, crashing through then landing on something huge, warm, with a gamey smell she knew.

The moose bolted up, throwing her to the side, thundered off into the woods. The breath knocked out of her, Leah lay until she could breathe, panting, whimpering.

She made it to her feet, ran again. The road. Doris's old house. Empty, dark. She slowed, confused at the sight of snow. It was too warm for snow. But snow was falling, swirling, huge flakes dancing and resting gently all around, mesmerizing her. In moments, it covered the ground.

She did not feel the cold, kept moving toward a place she had always felt safe. The meadow.

A flash, radiation of light for miles and miles around. The mountains thrust out of the gloom, showing themselves. Eerie. Leah felt all the hair on her body rise.

Energy vibrated within her at every white jolt. Lightning and snow? The sound of silence, so loud it hurt her ears.

༄

Terror, no place to hide now. She tries to remember something, anything that anyone may have taught her about being in the flats at a time like this.

"The trees," voice strangled, her breathing ragged.

The silence was alive all around her, terrifying her more than the sickening blue-white flashes.

It's like an awful dream.

Tripping, she almost falls into a blind dip in the muskeg. She curses herself for ending up in buckbrush, which she never must do.

The treeline. A flash. She reaches the trees. Huddling beneath the tallest. Alone and tiny. On this land she loves that is not hers.

A little wooden cross, leaning to the ground, shows in the next flash of light. The babies! She, Haywire. This is where they buried her babies! Dale Post's babies!

She feels the moss on her hands as she waters the tiny graves with tears. Haywire placing the cross, saying "Sorry" over and over.

She begins to cry now, then to pray. She uses every word of the language of this land she knows. She sings.

She feels the snowflakes in the silence, falling down on her. But they are not cold.

Smoke! Fire! Not snow, ash! The silence growing louder and louder still. Leah raises her head. Flash. The land is lit again.

Dead Indians! Mother! Why is she with them?

They stand, looking. Leah feels as though she has been struck by the next bolt. Energy shoots up her spine, and back down. She begins to call to them.

"Mother! Uncle Angus! Doris! Gramma!"

There are more dead Indians coming towards her. Mother holding Leah's baby in her arms. The buried child. It's cooing. Whose is the other baby that Uncle holds?

This was it. They were taking her with them. She is consumed by the unbearable longing to go.

Uncle Angus motions – *Come* – holds the baby out to her. Without hesitating, she stands, takes a first step toward them.

A memory flashes between lightning, plays like a film; she cannot stop it.

Haywire. Blood. The body.

Haywire speaking gently, as if to a child. "Leah, go inside, I'll take care of this."

Haywire coming to her later. She feeling as if her face is stone, staring out at the lake, blood still running all over her face, all down her front, pooling on the floor. He sits looking the floor for a long time.

"Listen – you have to listen to me. He's dead, Leah."

She is silent, still cannot move.

"Leah, he's a cop – and I know you didn't mean to, but you killed him. Nobody can know what happened here. Everyone knows you hated him.

"There's a lot of places here a man will never be found. A lot of places where a truck can disappear. We can't ever talk about this again, Leah. We can't ever tell anyone. Ever.

"Now come with me, I'll need your help."

<p>

Here in the flats, now a final flash. Explosion. Burning wood. Blinding in the black. She falls, allows a slow and peaceful darkness to envelop her.

Leah sees the light through her eyelids. Feels the frigid white morning air on her skin. Confused, asks herself what is she doing out here? She sits up, hand to her head to still the thundering.

Feels an old scar on her scalp. The kiss of the axe. Charcoal is all over her. The tree she had been standing under blown to bits all over the ground – now small black pieces all around her.

She is covered by a familiar old blanket. Ash covers it. She sees the canteen of water beside her. She drinks deeply. Cool on cracked lips. The slush soothing on a burning throat.

The pain in her head has receded a little. She coughs, stands staggering at first. Medicine. She gathers that which is holy, speaking her gratitude in the language of the land.

"Ah, *Gunalchish, Gunalchish Du xhuni*!

From a very old, glacial place deep within her core, tears of old, frigid pain melt. Drip down her face. A little girl place. A place high in alpine mountains where a tiny girl stands, looking down on what has been, what is, what will be.

"My medicine, Mother, Uncle, Gramma. It is all my medicine."

Her past, distilled from deep sadness, merges with her present here on this land, now. The Old Ones whisper within. The land speaks. The medicine sings its medicine song deep within her. The mountains witness. The earth holds her, gently. The water in the creek sings her name; the wind carries it far, wide.

Ravens catch it, fly across the meadows, calling it out.

She stands, breathing deeply, holds some of the lightning-fired medicine high in her hands.

Her life, with all its joy and ugliness, within her now. Before her eyes. She is now ready to see. She calls her name.

"Lightning Medicine Woman!"

Alive within her now, she feels all the power of lightning.

A nearby, and much loved voice says gently, "Are you ready now?"

She turns, sees her beloved Haywire, standing, looking at her, serious.

"Yes."

❧

FIRE WITHIN, Verse Two

Forged am I in pain, cooled am I in weeping
Forged am I in pain, cooled am I in weeping
And here am I, here am I, here am I
I'm a universe inside
The universe inside of me is uncharted territory
Each star is unnamed
And the outer world I see

Is but a reflection of what lives in me, in me, in me, in me, in me
Fire inside, fire inside
Fire inside, fire inside

ର

Leah smiles at Haywire and then at her growing belly. She closes her eyes. She opens them and writes.

ର

I can't believe it has been a year since I wrote in this. Maybe because too much has happened since Uncle's memorial.

Trying to be all of who I should be has taken two years.

I piss people off by being who I am. I laugh a lot. I have a bad habit of stepping on people's last nerve.

I also know this is a sacred medicine.

Rage and fear are also sacred. I inspire a lot of it in people when I accidentally ask them about the most painful secret of their existence.

On the upside, I can also break tension like a hot damn. Have a way of making people laugh without trying to, without meaning to. Another very sacred medicine,

The spirits who come to me now are very badly behaved. I wouldn't have them any other way. The holy ones are too predictable. If spirits are meant all pious and spiritual, mine are like crows cawing their smartass comments.

I was in the hospital. After the North. The first time. Close to death. I knew this by the wildly increased number of spirit visits.

The first was my dead friend Rayne, who died in the early days of AIDS. He came running in from the West. This makes perfect sense now; but I didn't know it back then. Here he comes, and he starts talking to me. I had no doubt it was him. His voice sounded like it was coming through water.

I said, "You sound different."

"Of course, I sound different. I'm dead, stupid!"

I had no doubt it was Rayne; it's exactly what he'd say.

Yeah, those badass spirits of mine. Love them. High entertainment. They don't politely wait for food and drink offerings.

I get, "What does a dead guy gotta do around here to get a decent cup of coffee? Or "I'm STARVING! Go get me an A&W hamburger. No!! Not that burger, the Uncle Burger, go get another one. And leave off the mustard and ketchup, I only want mayo. And I don't want Coke, I want Pepsi. And not that fountain stuff, it's crap. And not that stuff in the plastic bottle, it's never cold enough. Get it in a can. I like it better; and WHERE is the Fireball?" Fireball. Yup. My spirits like Fireball. You know. Cinnamon Whiskey.

There's that one who occasionally shows up and plants a kiss right on my lips.

And when they give advice, it's never just, "Do this, and all will be well." I get, "You are what I like to call 'wrong.'" Sarcastic spirits. They're the best.

Those Old Ones can be subtle – not! Always loaded with attitude. Once, they told me my ceremonial structure was loose. They waited until I was in there and it was right over on its side. They said, "So yeah, the poles are loose; just so ya know." It would have been nice to get a warning before I was in danger!

When those dead folks get wanting something and I haven't been paying attention (Excuse me for having a life!), they do things like pull my covers down really slowly, just until I wake up. And then they'll let me fall asleep again, and then down come the covers.

Last time, it was because I made Christmas candy and didn't leave it out and unwrapped for them. My offerings are always on a plate, and the sweets and such unwrapped. I had spent hours single-wrapping each of those caramels as gifts, and the house was fragrant with warm candy. Because I forgot to gift them, they came and did the slow cover pull. I yelled right there the first time, "Stop it, right now! Leave me alone! Go in the dining room and get some candy!"

Scared the hell out of Haywire. All he said was "Holy," and rolled back over.

Sometimes they'll just go right ahead and whack hard on the heater to get me up in the middle of the night for nothing. God, I hate that!

They have made me burst out laughing right in the middle of something. Like when I was doing some doctoring on somebody recently, they said, "Like we need your help." They were rolling their eyes at me. Try looking all serious and medicine womany under those circumstances!

And they really have no class whatsoever. They hang around even when I am intimate with Haywire. Once, they said, "Yell really loud, that's how you call your future children to you."

I burst out laughing. Try explaining that to a man. "I mean, really, Grammas, how could you?" And they just sat giggling in the corner.

But you know what? They've never said no to doctoring anyone, even if the person is drunk, or stoned. These badasses will tend to anyone who truly wants the help.

They are only ever serious when they doctor. They speak to me clearly, letting the person know what's at the heart of their sickness or trouble. They never joke when they're giving this advice. They are full of love and kindness. Unfailing.

Sometimes I ask the people I'm helping if they understand a message. I say, "I don't need to know why they're telling you this, but I just want to know if it makes sense." It always does.

I would only deal with these kind of spirits, if I had the choice. I didn't; they chose me. But if I had the choice? They would be my chosen every time. My fabulous Raven, darling, crazy dead Indians.

HOME

It is said
sub-Arctic glacial ice
melts, drips
from mountain peak
through moss to treeline.
Droplets unite to small stream,
lower, a creek
swelling, a river.
In perfect silence
rivers fall
winding south,
down, down,
still down through lush green,
over rock,
gathering the flavours of the land.
Flowing
miles and miles
finally home
to the sea.
The sea mists.
(Seasmoke to the Saltwater people).
Blows inland to mountains
that stand
from out of
the sea.
The mist gathered
by the
air currents
into cloud; blown high

into the atmosphere,
swirls and dances
to the North
on high winds.
Home
to the high country.
Home
to the alpine,
to glacial ice scape.
I have come
to this earth
from Water people
and I too
have come home,
to the mountains,
to the alpine,
glacial scape,
home
to the high country.
I live
with my deep love
of the deep North
that is the same
as my deep love
for the south sea.
I, part of them,
they, part of me.
One and the same.

Karen Lee White is a Northern Salish, Tuscarora, Chippewa, and Scots writer from Vancouver Island, British Columbia. She was adopted into the Daklaweidi clan of the Interior Tlingit/Tagish people, on whose land this story unfolds.

In 2017 Karen was awarded an Indigenous Art Award for Writing by the Hnatyshyn Foundation. Her work has appeared in Exile's *That Dammed Beaver: Canadian Humour; Laughs and Gaffes* anthology, *EXILE/ELQ* magazine, the collection of Indigenous writers *Impact, Colonialism in Canada*, and other literary journals. She has been commissioned as a playwright by theatres in Vancouver and Victoria, and was commissioned by the Banff Centre to produce a story for the "Fables of the 21st Century" special edition, released in 2018.

Acknowledgements:

*To my late mother, who always believed I was a writer
and read every scrap of paper she ever found with my writing on it.*

*To my late brother, who would have written
breathtaking work had he had the chance.*

To Witi Ihimaera, who said if I didn't write this book that he would.

*To Miles Morriseau, who did the first editing
and who believed in this work.*

To Bruce Meyer whose structural editing genius is unsurpassed.

*To Exile for their high standard of excellence,
and for believing in this piece.*

*To Linda Rogers for seeing the spark in the piece
and for support above and beyond the call of friendship.*

To my sister Leslie Gentile for soul-stirring vocals on "Fire Within."

*To Mark Preston for the stunning cover art
that captures the soul of the Yukon.*

*To my circle of loved ones, in this world and in the next.
You know who you are.*

Book + CD